GHOST MOON

KATHRYN KNIGHT

Wicked Whale
Publishing

Knight, Kathryn

Ghost Moon / by Kathryn Knight

Summary: When Lark Cavanaugh inherits an old family home, she finds new love...but her arrival awakens restless spirits and a deadly mystery.

ISBN: 978-1-7322522-5-7

Wicked Whale Publishing
P.O. Box 264
Sagamore Beach, MA 02562-9998

www.WickedWhalePublishing.com

Published in the United States of America

To my dad, for fostering my love of reading. Thank you for the many, many trips to the library. I miss you.

---

*L*ark Cavanaugh's stomach did a sluggish flip as she caught her first glimpse of Holloway House. Her foot eased off the gas pedal, slowing the car even beyond the crawling pace that had still registered every bump and rut along the unpaved road that passed as a driveway. *How was this her new home?* With a grimace, she urged the tires up a small hill, and the trees opened up to reveal the entire structure. It sat in a cleared slice of land that nature seemed eager to reclaim, surrounded on either side by encroaching scrub pines and tangled underbrush. A semi-circle in front of the house, dotted with weeds and the remnants of broken white shells, appeared to serve as a combination front yard and parking area, so she pulled to a stop along the edge.

The empty house would have looked creepy even if she hadn't known its history. In the evening shadows, the second story seemed to lean forward over the worn porch like a menacing beast leering at its prey. She shivered, blinking to clear the unsettling image. It was just her nerves working overtime. After all, the last ten days had been a traumatic whirlwind of shocking revelations and emotional turmoil. And now she was about to move into an abandoned house that the entire population of this small town believed to be haunted. It was a good thing she didn't believe in ghosts. Deceitful, selfish people...yes, she believed in that. Now more than ever. Ghosts, no.

She tightened her grip on the steering wheel, and her gaze drifted to the bare ring finger of her left hand. Closing her eyes, she blew out a breath, gritting her teeth against the new image that flashed behind her lids. That disturbing memory was seared into her brain forever, and she couldn't chalk this one up to nerves. Another wave of nausea burned through her belly as she cut the engine. *Don't think about it.*

A plaintive mewling brought her back to the present, and she threaded her fingers through the metal bars of the cat carrier on the passenger seat. "I know," she murmured, stroking the corner of Preston's soft mouth. "It was a long drive." Six hours, in fact, from New York City to the town of Truro on Cape Cod, in a borrowed car that felt like it might break apart at any minute. She could relate.

No. She would not let this beat her. It felt as though the fates were testing her, hammering at her defenses in an attempt to shatter her into pieces. But she'd been through worse, and the prolonged nightmare of the last week and a half certainly wasn't going to be the thing that brought her to her knees. At least not permanently. She would move into this strange, isolated house she'd suddenly inherited and regroup.

She would come out stronger. "Right, Pres?" she whispered into the silence, knowing full well her cat couldn't read her thoughts, and couldn't answer even if he could. But she may as well get used to talking to herself until she could unload this place and get back to the city.

The lawyer had warned her it would be difficult to sell, for a number of reasons. The house sat on two acres, with a river running through the woods, but it wasn't directly on the ocean or the bay. The town was sparsely populated and secluded. While the property had been maintained by a trust, the interior had been closed up since Lark's great aunt Joan had moved into a nursing home ten years ago, before passing away last month.

And then there were the rumors swirling around the house, labeling it haunted and cursed. Apparently at least two of her distant relatives had died here, the wife in a tragic accident, the husband by suicide after a dark descent into grief and madness.

That had been 70 years ago, though. Every old house in Massachusetts probably had a grisly death or two in its past. Many of these towns had first been settled in the late 1600s. Homes with that kind of history had to come with a fair share of tragedies.

A movement caught the corner of her eye, and her gaze snapped up to one of the second-floor windows. A pale, gauzy face peered out at her from behind the cloudy glass. She gasped, her muscles tensing as her hand flew to her mouth. *Who was in the house?*

She blinked, and the face disappeared. Or, rather, the

mirage her exhausted mind had conjured disappeared. Nothing was ever there, she silently reassured herself, sliding her damp palm down over her racing heart. *I'm imagining things, that's all.* But as she craned forward, searching the upstairs window through the car windshield, she thought she saw the curtains ripple in the falling dusk.

Great. The stories were getting to her already. Rubbing her eyes, she heaved a long sigh. She needed to get inside, let poor Preston out of the crate, and put her feet up. Unpacking could wait, except for maybe the cat food. And the half-full bottle of wine she'd brought along in the cooler.

Warm June air and an uncanny silence greeted her as she opened the driver's side door. The absence of honking horns, exhaust fumes, and harried pedestrians was nearly as jarring as the imaginary face in the window. Climbing out of the car, she stretched her arms above her head, then combed her fingers through her heavy auburn hair. As she rolled an elastic tie off her wrist and twisted it around a low ponytail, she surveyed the packed backseat of the car.

It wasn't all that much, even adding in the bags in the trunk, when you considered this jumbled collection of boxes and crates basically represented her entire life. Some of the furniture in the apartment was technically hers, but she couldn't have fit it, and besides, she didn't really want anything that reminded her of the place she'd called home for three years right now. If she decided she needed something, she could deal with that when she returned the car in the middle of July, when the friend of a friend who'd allowed her to use it would return from an overseas trip. How she would get back to the

Cape again was still an unsolved problem…but maybe, if she were really lucky, she'd find an interested buyer, and she wouldn't have to come back at all.

"Not likely," she grumbled, opening the passenger door to retrieve the cat carrier. Preston made a low guttural sound in response. Grabbing a duffle bag with her free hand, she trudged toward the house, praying the key would be where it was supposed to be. The lawyer had assured her a local realtor with a copy would come by and hide it for her.

It was there beside the door, tucked beneath an old planter filled with gray dirt and a few tenacious weeds. She slid the key into the lock, frowning at the slight tremble in hand. But a little anxiety was warranted in a situation like this, right? Long trip, new—*old*—house, and a growing need to locate the bathroom.

She twisted the knob, surprised at how easily the old metal turned beneath her sweaty palm. Almost as if someone on the other side of the door was helping. *God.* Rolling her eyes at the ridiculous thought, she wiped her hands on her shorts and picked up the bag and carrier before crossing the threshold.

Part of her had imagined she'd find furniture shrouded in dingy white sheets and chandeliers draped in dusty cobwebs. But the inside of the house appeared fairly normal, despite the dated décor and the stale air. An artificial floral scent struggled to mask a damp, musty odor, and Lark's gaze found an air freshener plugged into a socket by the base of the stairs. A wave of gratitude swept over her at the realtor's thoughtful gesture. But the real test would be the electricity and water—

she'd been assured by the lawyer the utilities would be on by the time she arrived.

She held her breath as she flicked the switch beside the door, and let it out with relief as the light above her head brightened the entryway. The switch beside it lit up the living area to her left. Phew. Now for the bathroom. She shut the front door behind her and set the carrier down first, opening the door. "Come on out and check out our new digs, Pres," she called as she hurried through the living room into the kitchen. The open floor plan was basically a large rectangle, and she found a tiny bathroom where the kitchen led into the dining room.

The running water lifted her spirits, and she searched the cabinets for a shallow bowl to fill with water for Preston. Surprisingly, the appliances didn't look as obsolete as she'd pictured. Someone must have made some changes over the years.

Returning to the foyer, she scanned the area for Preston. Her brows drew together as she failed to find his familiar gray and white form slinking through the new environment, tail twitching as he cautiously sniffed every inch.

"Pres?" she called, the word hanging in the heavy air. She squatted down by the cat carrier, wincing as several joints cracked like dried twigs. She needed a warm bath and a soft bed. Her 25-year-old body felt ancient after spending over a week sleeping on an uncomfortable couch.

There he was, still huddled in the carrier, his body pressed as far against the back of the plastic crate as possible. Yellow-green eyes glittered, unblinking, from the dark interior.

Weird. Why wouldn't he want to get out of his cramped quarters, now that he could? She cooed at him, trying to coax him out, but when he wouldn't budge, she set down the water and stood back up before her stiff muscles locked her into a permanent crouch. "Suit yourself," she murmured with a shrug. Maybe he just needed time to acclimate...time to feel safe here.

A shudder ran through her as the phantom face in the window flashed through her mind. *How much time would she need?* Hopefully, not too much...she was bone-tired. Just your imagination, she reminded herself as she went back outside to grab a few more things. Still, she avoided looking up at the windows on her way back toward the house.

Once she'd set up a food bowl and a litter tray near the carrier—still occupied by her strangely cautious cat—she climbed the staircase to check out the bedrooms. A small landing midway up connected another set of stairs leading to the kitchen. At the top, a section of the bannister continued in each direction along the narrow hallway.

She paused, hand resting on the wooden finial of the newel post, and glanced back down to see if Preston was following her. Nope. Shaking her head slightly, she peeked into the bathroom across the hall, then turned and made her way to the door at the right end of the hallway. The wooden floorboards creaked beneath her footsteps, the sound eerily magnified in the thick silence. After so many years of city living, where noises drifted from the bustling streets and the neighboring apartments at every hour, the quiet here was surreal. Utter and complete, it reminded her how alone she was now. And in so

KATHRYN KNIGHT

many more ways than just being in this creepy isolated house in this tiny isolated town.

She set her jaw against the impending wave of self-pity and pushed open the door with more force than necessary. A master bedroom greeted her, sparsely furnished but quaint in its vintage style. There was no master bath, but another doorway led to an adjoining room outfitted as a study. She wandered in, feeling a bit like she was stepping back in time.

A heavy wooden desk sat in the center, framed black and white photos tucked between paperweights and leather accessories. Picking one up, she blew on the dusty glass. A couple and a child she didn't recognize. Probably relatives, but her connection to this part of the family was distant—the house had landed with her through a series of strange circumstances and tragedies. But this room would be a treasure trove if she wanted to learn more about her mother's side of the family.

Setting the picture down, she swept her gaze over to a set of portraits on the wall. A stern-looking couple occupied matching frames, the man wearing a white clerical collar. Above the two portraits hung a large cross, and Lark recalled that her relative John Holloway had been the local pastor. He and his wife, Martha, were the ones who had first lived in this house after having it built in the late 1940s.

Below the portraits, shelves held rows of books and boxes. In the corners of the room, evidence of more recent inhabitants sat piled on chairs—games, puzzles, and stacks of mail. Lark checked the date on a magazine cover. April 2003. Maybe the fashions would be back in style at this point.

The windows along the far wall overlooked the back of the

property, and she paused to enjoy the view. It really *was* peaceful. A low wooden deck stretched out from the kitchen, and beyond that, a gentle hill rolled down to the tree line. The narrow river that marked the property line wound its way through the brush and pitch pines, and beyond that, she could just make out the back of her closest neighbor's house at the top of the opposing rise.

A wave of dizziness swept over her, and she rubbed her forehead. She needed to eat and rest. Backtracking, she left the master bedroom and followed the hallway down to the other end and the two additional rooms.

She opened the door on her right and peeked into a smaller bedroom with a backyard view similar to the one from the study. As she closed that door and turned to the one directly across from it, she hesitated, chewing on her lip. This was the room with the front-facing windows. The room that had appeared to have an occupant staring out at her as she arrived.

Her fingers trembled slightly as she closed them around the knob. Silly. And yet…what if there *was* someone in there? Not necessarily a ghost, but an intruder…

Should she go grab a weapon? With a small shake of her head, she dismissed the idea. If someone was here, and did intend harm, he or she could have easily snuck up on her earlier. Pulling in a deep breath, she eased the door open.

Her eyes shot to the far window. No one there. The thud of her heartbeat pounded in her ears as she scanned the rest of the room. It appeared empty, but there were twin beds and a small closet to investigate before she could declare the house unoccupied.

As she took a tentative step forward, a wave of cold air swirled around her, and she tensed, her muscles tightening, her breath catching. *What the hell?* Her gaze snapped back to the window. Closed. Goosebumps prickled her skin as she swiveled her head around, searching for a source.

A mournful sigh rustled in her ear, and her frozen body suddenly came to life, her limbs flailing defensively as she stumbled sideways. Jumping onto one of the beds, she scrambled backwards until her spine slammed into the headboard, pulling her knees into her chest to make herself as small as possible.

She stared, unblinking, into the empty room, her heart pounding so hard she was surprised it wasn't banging through the wooden bedframe into the wall. But no one appeared in the doorway, no one emerged from the closet. No footsteps retreated down the hall. Slowly, her racing heart decelerated as rational explanations began to break the surface of her fear.

Just the wind, curling and moaning through the joints and cracks of an old house.

But there hadn't been a trace of a breeze when she'd arrived.

She bit her lip against the defiant inner voice. Truro was basically a narrow strip of land surrounded by the Atlantic Ocean on one side and Cape Cod Bay on the other. Strange weather patterns probably popped up all the time around here.

Pulling in a shuddering breath, she unfolded herself and eased her torso over the edge of the bed. She was going to have to pull up the bed skirt—on both beds—and check, just for peace of mind. It was stupid to think a gust of chilly air or a noise beside her ear could materialize from beneath a bed, but at the same time, the image of the shadowy face in the window continued to flit through her mind like photos sliding across a screen.

She craned her neck down, grasping the white cotton with trembling fingers, gathering her courage. What if that face leered back at her when she peered down, its empty eyes piercing hers as a bony claw shot forward to seize her throat?

Oh, God. Biting back the scream rising in anticipation, she yanked the bed skirt up and dropped her head far enough to scan beneath the box spring. Just bare floorboards, unless you counted a trio of ancient dust bunnies hiding in the shadows. Exhaling, she let the material drop as she hauled herself up.

One more bed to check. And the closet. Steeling herself, she repeated the process, feeling slightly ridiculous by the time she wrenched open the closet door with a simultaneous jump backwards. Only a few empty hangers, a faded ironing board, and cardboard boxes too small to conceal an intruder.

With a sharp nod of her head, she turned and hurried out of the chilly room, scowling at the quaking tremors in her legs. *Everything's fine.* But she shut the door to the front bedroom firmly behind her before she made her way back downstairs.

---

*S*he awoke to a strange sound, the muffled thumps pulling her from restless dreams. Blinking in the darkness, she stilled beneath the covers. *The cat?* It must be Preston, engaging in some nocturnal exploration of his new digs. He sure wasn't doing much during the daytime. In fact, once he had finally ventured out of his carrier, he'd holed up beneath her bed, and he'd barely seemed to move from his new spot in the three days they'd been here, at least as far as she'd noticed. By the end of the second day, she'd moved his litter box and food and water into the upstairs bathroom, but it didn't seem like he was taking advantage of the proximity of either one. His food appeared untouched, the litter box clean. He must be going somewhere else in the house...that was going to be a fun clean-up job when she discovered where. But concern for him outweighed any tinges of annoyance. The back-to-back moves—first to her friend Madison's apartment, then here—had really shaken her sweet boy up, and she felt terrible.

At least it sounded like he was up and about now. She strained her ears, listening for his movements as she shifted on the lumpy mattress. The house was quiet now; even the soft hum of insects drifting through the open windows seemed to have ceased. Something about the sudden hush felt threatening, as though a storm just over the horizon was about to unleash its fury. Pulling in a shallow breath, she gripped the edge of the sheet as a thread of unease snaked along her spine.

A soft moan rippled through the silence, and she froze, fear surging through her in sharp, sickening waves. She lay motionless, her lungs trembling, her mind reeling. What the hell was that? Whatever it was did not sound feline. *Or human.* The rush of her heartbeat filled her ears as she slowly craned her neck, raising her head a few inches from the pillow. She swept her gaze around the room, searching the melting shadows and murky corners. Acid burned the back of her throat as she waited helplessly for a figure to break away from the layers of darkness.

Nothing materialized, and she forced her arm to reach for the lamp on the nightstand. Light. She needed light. Her shaking fingers finally found the tiny plastic knob, and she turned it, offering a silent prayer. It had worked earlier. *Please, God...let it work now.*

With a faint click, a cone of light illuminated the corner of the room, and she let out a slow breath. Okay. Swallowing hard, she eased up against the headboard, keeping her body still while continuing to scan the room for movement. Pieces of furniture came into focus, the reassuring shapes remaining stationary. Aside from the rasp of her shallow breaths, the house was quiet. Had she conjured the thudding noises on the edge of a dream? It was a comforting thought, but she was certain she'd been awake when she'd heard that moan. *Just like the first night, in the other bedroom*, her inner voice reminded her with unnecessary harshness. She fought back a shudder as her eyes darted among the trio of doors leading to the closet, the study, and the hallway. There was no avoiding it. She was going to have to investigate if she planned on getting any more sleep tonight.

Gritting her teeth, she threw off the covers and summoned her courage. First up, more light. With a bit of awkward gymnastics, she launched herself away from the bed and anything that might be lurking underneath, then raced toward the light switch on the wall.

She heaved a sigh of relief as the bulbs of the ceiling fixture blinked to life. Okay. The door to the hallway was already partially open, to allow Preston access to his food and litter box. And what she had heard—the thumps, anyway—had certainly been the cat. As for the eerie moan that seemed to come from the air beside her ear, well…that was probably Preston too. The acoustics of the house had just distorted the sound, changed it into something mournful and otherworldly.

As she opened the door further, the bedroom light spilled out into the hallway, and she followed it, hugging her arms across her chest. "Pres?" she called out, her voice a dry croak.

Only silence answered her at first, until a plaintive mewl from behind her chilled her blood. *That* was Preston, no question. But...where was he? She spun on her heel, racing back into the master bedroom. Dropping to the floor with enough force to send a jolt of pain through her knees, she yanked up the comforter and peered under the bed.

Preston's familiar form sprawled beneath the box spring, but the position of his body told her something wasn't right. Dread poured into her belly, thick and viscous. She reached for him, whispering his name as she stretched her arm beneath the bed frame. When her fingers closed on the scruff of his neck, she pulled him toward her, and his failure to fight sent a fresh bolt of alarm through her veins. He slid across the wood floor like a sack of stones, putting up no resistance as she freed him from under the bed.

He remained on his side, eyes half-closed, pink tongue hanging out. When she ran a hand over his body, he emitted another guttural moan, and she snatched her fingers away and clapped them over her mouth. *Oh, God.*

She needed to get him to a vet. Right away. But this wasn't the city...was there even a vet in this little town? One that was open in the middle of the night? Why hadn't she thought to check on that before they arrived? Her mind reeled as she scrambled sideways to grab her phone from the nightstand.

"Hang on, Pres," she murmured, her thumbs flying over the screen. *Please.* Holding her breath, she scrolled through the results of her search. There. One vet office in this town: Truro Veterinary Clinic. She glanced at the time as she hit the call button. The chances of it being open at 1:20 a.m. were slim, but she crossed her fingers anyway as she gently stroked them over Preston's head.

Dismay filled her chest when a recorded message picked up, but then the miracle she'd prayed for arrived—a number to call in case of emergency. Dr. Holt. Jumping to her feet, she sprinted into the office and scribbled the number on an envelope before she could forget it. Then she quickly ended the first call and made the second, squeezing her eyes shut as rings pealed on the other end of the line.

"Holt."

She slumped with relief, leaning against the desk for support. "Dr. Holt? Oh, thank God. I'm new in town, and my cat is really sick. He didn't take the move very well, and he hasn't really been eating. And now he's not moving. I can tell he's in pain, he's making horrible noises." The words tumbled out in a hectic rush, her voice rising in pitch with each rapid sentence. She paused for a breath, pacing back into the bedroom to stand over Preston's limp body.

"Okay. How old is the cat?" the doctor asked, his deep voice rough with sleep, but calm.

"Um…he's a rescue, so I can't say for sure." She squatted down to make sure Preston was still breathing. His belly appeared rigid, but his side rose and fell in labored gasps. "He's about five or six now—not that old."

"Any previous issues?" In the background, drawers opened and closed.

She shook her head. "No."

"Does he go outdoors?"

She shook her head again, aware on some level he couldn't see her gestures, but unable to control the instincts. "He's an indoor-only cat, at least as long as I've had him, which is about three years."

"Okay, do you know where the office is?"

"I can find it."

"I can be there in about ten minutes. I'll see you there."

Oh, thank God. Tears pressed against her eyes as her throat swelled, and she barely managed to choke out a raspy "thank you" before a sob broke free. She ended the call quickly, hoping he hadn't heard it. Then she pulled the vet office address back up and loaded directions. Ten minutes...the same amount of time as it would take him. She needed to get her poor cat into the carrier and leave immediately.

As she flew down the stairs to grab the carrier, she suddenly realized she was only wearing a worn T-shirt and boy-short underwear. No time to change. Panting with effort and fear, she raced back into the bedroom and grabbed a pair of cut-off jean shorts from the laundry basket. Once she'd yanked them on, she wrapped Preston in a towel and gently slid him into the carrier, grimacing as he let out a weak yowl.

Twelve minutes later, she was there. The vet office looked more like a large house, sitting back from the road with a parking lot in front, but the front light was on, and a motorcycle stood in a spot by the door. Seemed a strange choice of transportation for a veterinarian, but the sign told her she was in the right place.

She wrapped her arms around the carrier in an awkward embrace to avoid jostling Preston, slamming the car door with her foot and hurrying toward the building. A tall form opened the door for her, and a fresh wave of relief swam through her. He would help them.

As she climbed the two steps, she looked up to thank him, but the words caught in her throat as she stared at his face. My God, he was handsome. And young. Maybe her age, or a few years older. Certainly not what she'd been expecting a small-town vet to look like. Suddenly the bike out front made a little more sense, and an uninvited image of this hot man riding it flashed through her mind.

"I'm Dr. Holt," he said as he lifted the carrier out of her arms.

His introduction broke into her dazed stupor, and shame flooded her veins as she yanked her attention back to her suffering cat. Jesus. What was wrong with her? How could her mind go there at a time like this? How could her mind go there at all, after everything that had happened in New York?

She dragged her fingers through her hair in an effort to push the intruding thoughts away, ignoring the primal part of her brain reminding her she hadn't even brushed her teeth before she jumped in the car, much less the mass of tangles falling around her shoulders.

"Thank you," she managed, before realizing that wasn't the correct response. "I mean...I'm Lark Cavanaugh. Thank you for seeing us so late."

He nodded. "I'm going to take him back, Ms. Cavanaugh. Go ahead and have a seat."

"Lark. I mean, please call me Lark. You'll let me know?"

"As soon as I can." He disappeared through a door behind

the front desk, and she was left standing there, twisting her hands.

She paced the floor for a few minutes, wishing for a mirror, or maybe a mint at least. God, what was the matter with her? Who cared? Hopefully, Dr. Holt would fix her cat, and then she'd never see the guy again.

He emerged from the back room, and she spun around, her heart skipping out an erratic beat. *Please, please let him be okay.*

"Your cat..." he paused, a crease forming between his clear blue eyes. "What's his name?"

"Preston."

"Preston. He has a urethral obstruction. His urinary tract is blocked, which is a life-threatening condition."

Her hand flew to her mouth. "Will he..." She swallowed hard, tried again. "Can you save him?"

"I need to sedate him and catheterize him. Hopefully that will work. If not, surgery is required. Either way, he'll be here for a few days while we monitor him. It's not going to be inexpensive."

Closing her eyes, she blew out a breath. Every cell in her body was screaming that it didn't matter, but she needed to know. "How much?"

"It will depend how things go, but you'll be looking at $1,000 minimum." He ran a hand over his jaw, shadowed with the night's stubble.

A thousand minimum probably meant a lot more, but what choice did she have? None. "I'll find the money. Whatever it takes," she added, her voice warbling. "He's all I have."

Something flashed across his face, and she realized she probably sounded pathetic, sharing the fact that a cat was literally the most important presence in her life. Then again, this man had dedicated his life to saving animals, so maybe he understood. Her gaze dropped inadvertently to his ring finger. Bare. But she'd pulled him out of bed in the middle of the night.

"Okay," he said gently, taking her elbow and steering her toward the desk. "We can always set up a payment plan too. But right now, I need you to fill out a few forms while I get some things ready."

She fought to ignore the warm tingle the touch of his hand left behind. Apparently, her body was dealing with the stress in some very inappropriate ways. Biting down on her lip, she accepted the clipboard and took a seat in the waiting area.

He returned in a few minutes, and she jumped up and crossed the room to meet him halfway. He was now wearing dark blue scrubs in place of the jeans and T-shirt he'd arrived in. His dark brown hair had been pushed back off his forehead, but the thick waves remained tousled from sleep and a motorcycle ride. A suntan set off his strong, chiseled features and full lips. He gave her a tight smile as she handed him the forms.

"All set," she said, resisting the urge to run past him to check on Preston.

"He's hanging in there."

She flushed, twisting the pen in her fingers. Obviously she was easy to read.

"One of my vet techs should be here any minute. We'll get him sedated and on pain meds, then go from there to clear the obstruction." He gestured with the clipboard. "One of us will contact you at the number you gave us."

"Oh." The thought of leaving hadn't even occurred to her. She gripped the pen so hard her nails dug into her palm. "Um...I was thinking I would stay?"

He tilted his head, his brows knitting together. "That's not necessary."

"No, I realize that," she said hurriedly, hoping he didn't think she was suggesting he was incompetent. Her presence in the waiting room certainly wouldn't make a difference in the outcome of the procedure, and yet, she felt she needed to be there. The idea of going back to that spooky house by herself held less appeal than curling up on the stiff couch here, where Preston was. And a nagging voice in the back of her mind kept reminding her that *something* had made those noises that had awoken her in the first place—and it probably hadn't been her sick, incapacitated cat. "Still, I'd like to stay, if that's okay." She flicked her gaze over to the waiting area.

The door swung open, and a woman with wild hair and paw-print scrubs rushed inside. "Got here as fast as I could," she announced between rapid breaths.

"Thanks, Diane." Dr. Holt set the clipboard down on the front desk and tipped his chin toward the back. "Let's get started." Casting a glance back to Lark, he lifted a shoulder. "You can stay if you like. Make yourself comfortable. I'll come let you know how it goes." He followed Diane through the door in the back and disappeared.

There was nothing she could do now but wait. Exhaustion swept over her in a sudden, fierce tidal wave, and she staggered over to the couch, her body collapsing onto the rigid foam cushions. She bent forward, dropping her head into her hands, wishing she had someone to talk to. Someone she was close enough to call in the middle of the night; someone who wouldn't mind being woken up to listen to her fears and share her worry. But there was no one left who fit in that category. Certainly not Brittney or Nathan. Her stomach turned just thinking of them. Madison had already done enough for her, putting her up in her tiny studio apartment for over a week. And her parents... She shuddered, swallowing back a sob. Her father had taught her to be strong. Self-reliant. All she could do now was sit here and hope that Dr. Holt could save her sweet cat.

With a sigh, she straightened up, realizing she didn't even have her phone with her if she *were* going to make a call. It was still sitting on the passenger seat of her borrowed car. She debated going outside to get it, then shrugged and sank back into the corner of the couch. Closing her eyes, she sent up a silent prayer to anyone who was listening.

3

"*L*ark?"

A warm hand touched her arm, and she surfaced from sleep, momentarily confused as to where she was and why she was jammed into an uncomfortable ball on a small couch. *The vet's office!* She lurched up into a sitting position, barely noticing the fiery spasms of pain radiating from her cramped muscles and stiff joints.

Blinking, she brought the doctor's impossibly handsome face into focus. The soft glow of natural light filled the waiting room. How long had she been asleep? What did that mean in terms of her cat? "Preston?" was all she managed to croak out.

"He's doing great," Dr. Holt said reassuringly. Crouching down to her level, he handed her a bottle of water. "You seemed...well, like you really needed some sleep. So I decided to let you have a few hours even though the procedure was over a while ago."

Blood heated her cheeks as she pictured herself conked out

on a waiting room couch, knees pinned to her chest, face slack with apparently obvious exhaustion. God, what if she was snoring? She scrubbed at her greasy face, reminding herself it didn't matter. What mattered was Preston was okay.

"We sedated him, gave him pain meds, and catheterized him. I was able to clear the blockage, so now we just have to monitor him for a bit."

She nodded, suddenly processing the water bottle in her hand. A warm rush of gratitude filled her chest as she twisted the cap open. This man had saved her cat, let her sleep in his waiting room, and then thought to bring her water. "Oh, thank you so much, Doctor. That's great news. When can I bring him home?"

"Like I said, we're going to need to monitor him, at least for another day." He stood back up, gesturing toward the back of the room. "We're not really set up to be a 24-hour-facility, but I think I can cobble together a few overnight shifts. It would hardly be the first time."

She took a swig from the bottle, hoping the water would help wash the sour taste from her mouth. "Are you sure? I would really appreciate that." Capping the bottle, she pushed herself up to stand across from him.

"We'll make it work."

Guilt pricked at her, but she couldn't bring herself to deny the kindness. What would the alternative be—taking Preston to a true emergency clinic in another town? She couldn't even imagine the cost associated with that. Not that this would be cheap, either. But at least it was local, and they were already here. "Thank you," she repeated, locking eyes with him for a moment before she cast her gaze over his shoulder, toward the doors beyond the front desk.

"You can come see him, if you'd like." He turned and led her towards the back.

She attempted to smooth her tangled hair with her free hand as she followed him, glancing at the clock on the wall. Almost 6:00 a.m.

"We'll call you if there are any complications. No news is good news. But you can certainly call at the end of business hours today to check in."

She wondered if this was a subtle attempt to make sure she was leaving now. Unable to resist, she feigned confusion. "Oh, I just figured I'd stick around. It'll be naptime soon anyway." Glancing back toward the waiting area, she added, "What time is breakfast?"

He laughed, a deep, pleasant sound. "Buffet service starts at 6:30. All you can eat."

She chuckled with him as he pushed the door open. "Don't worry, I'll get out of your hair after I say goodbye to Preston. I don't imagine it's good for business to have a frightening-looking woman sleeping on your couch."

He stood back to allow her to pass, his gaze lingering on her face for a few beats. "Definitely not frightening." The corners of his mouth twitched into the hint of a smile as he cleared his throat. "But, yes, we do try to discourage clients sleeping in the waiting area during business hours."

"I get it." She caught sight of Preston, sleeping in a cage along the back wall. Her chest twisted with an overwhelming mix of relief and heartbreak as she took in his shaved legs and plastic cone. Before she rushed toward him, she turned back to Dr. Holt, nearly bumping into him. "Thank you, so much, for saving him. And please tell everyone else—the tech that came in last night, the ones who stay tonight—I said thank you. I'm truly grateful." Blinking back the sting of tears, she hurried across the room.

4

_____

*S*he bolted upright in bed, the series of thumps that had awakened her still ringing in her ears. Fumbling for the light, she pulled the covers against her chest, as though that could offer some protection against whatever had made the noises. *What the hell was it?* She scanned the room, her pulse skittering in jagged bursts. Why was this happening to her? Hadn't she been through enough?

Nothing in the bedroom appeared to be the source of the disturbance, but her instincts told her the sounds had originated from somewhere else in the house. And it definitely wasn't the cat this time—he was still at the vet's.

Reaching for her phone, she sucked in a breath as she noticed the time...1:06 a.m. Exactly the same time she'd been awoken last night. She glanced back up to the hallway door as she jabbed at the screen, pulling up the keypad just in case she needed to call 911. In addition to occurring at the same time, though, whatever she'd just heard sounded similar to last night's mysterious disturbance, and that hadn't been an intruder. Not a living one, anyway.

As if on cue, a haunting moan shivered through the air. Her lungs froze as a fresh spike of fear pierced her chest. *Oh, God.* There really was something wrong with this house. Fighting the urge to dive back under the covers and hide, she slowly climbed out of bed, unsure what exactly she was going to do. Check the house, for starters, she decided. Her mind was still begging for a more reasonable, less terrifying scenario. A quirky appliance, maybe?

With each tentative step, she paused, waiting for something else to happen. As she made her way into the hall, a chill enveloped her, and she crossed her arms, rubbing the goose-bumps rising on her skin. Below her, the stairway unfurled into shadows cast by the upper hall light.

A loud crash rang out behind her, and she jumped, a scream tearing from her lips. She spun around, searching for the source even as she backed toward the top step. The slice of bedroom she could see through the doorway remained empty. She kept her eyes trained on the open door as she inched backwards down the first few steps; then she turned and bolted the rest of the way down, focused only on getting closer to an escape route.

Nothing chased her down the stairs, and she paused with her hand on the knob of the front door, huffing out ragged breaths. What were her options now? Was she going to sleep in her car?

Maybe you can go back to the vet's office couch, some crazed voice in the back of her head suggested, and she fought down a bubble of hysterical laughter. How did she get herself into this? The answer came to her, complete with vicious images, and she deflated, sinking back into the door. Her options really were limited. She literally had nowhere to go, and now, with a hefty vet bill in her future, a hotel room was more out of reach than ever.

Time to fall back, once again, on the lessons her father had always instilled in her. She needed to rely on herself. With a heavy sigh, she pushed away from the door and crossed the living room, snapping on lights along the way. When she reached the fireplace, she examined the dusty iron tools, selecting a dangerous-looking poker.

Climbing the stairs, she wielded the weapon in front of her chest, her heartbeat thudding in her ears. Nothing appeared out of place in the bedroom, but she checked any possible hiding places thoroughly while keeping an eye on the door to the adjoining study.

For some reason, she didn't like that room. It didn't make her quite as uneasy as that front bedroom on the other end of the hall, but it still felt...off. Initially, she'd thought it was the clutter, but maybe there was another reason for her discomfort.

She approached the study slowly, brandishing the poker like a sword, and scanned the room from the doorway. Her gaze caught on an empty space on the wall, then dropped to the framed picture on the floor. The portrait of the man—Pastor John, presumably—now lay face-down on the wood floorboards. Above, the woman who must have been his wife still stared out from the matching frame, her stern expression suddenly appearing almost accusatory.

Okay. At least here was a physical cause for the crash—a picture had fallen off the wall. The adrenaline drained from her body like air from a leaky balloon, and she sagged against the door frame, the tip of the poker hitting the floor with a dull thud.

Or maybe it was pulled off the wall, on purpose. Although there was a logical explanation for this latest scare lying in front of her, it was tough to deny the timing...the portrait had fallen right after a second night's worth of mysterious noises and disembodied moans. She still didn't know what to make of that, and she really didn't want to think about the possibilities right now. Her mind felt foggy and her head ached. She needed to at least try to get some rest, as unlikely as that might be.

Not up here, though. She shut the door to the study behind her, and then the bedroom door as well as she trudged back downstairs. At the landing, she followed the back staircase the rest of the way down into the kitchen.

It felt safer in here, with the bright lights and the close proximity to the sliding glass door leading out to the deck. The lock on the screen door was broken, but she pushed the slider open anyway to let in some air. At this point, she was less afraid of what might be out in the dark woods than whatever was in the house.

With a sigh, she examined the contents of the fridge, eventually pulling out the milk. When she was a child, her mother used to make her a mug of warm milk when she couldn't sleep.

A pang of grief flowed through her as she poured her own mug and heated it in the microwave.

She eased into a chair at the round kitchen table, propping her elbows on the laminated wood surface and cradling her chin. A pile of paperwork sat in the center, and she studied the top sheet: her new work schedule.

After leaving the vet's office this morning—yesterday morning, technically—she'd returned home to get a few hours more sleep on an actual bed. Not surprisingly, though, her muscles had rebelled further from their time on the couch, seizing into tight, painful knots. Once she'd lurched downstairs and had a late breakfast, she'd brought her yoga mat out onto the deck and spent an hour stretching in the sunshine.

Once she'd showered, she pulled on her favorite summer dress, a sleeveless lime sheath that brought out the green of her eyes. She dusted bronzer across her cheeks and twisted her red hair into a casual knot, then headed back into town. She stopped at the vet's office first, to check on Preston, annoyed with the little flip her stomach did in anticipation of seeing Dr. Holt. He must have been at lunch, or in an exam room, because she didn't run into him, and the resulting surge of disappointment irritated her further. What was wrong with her? She was fresh off a broken engagement. To a complete jerk, as it turned out. She shouldn't even be noticing a man right now, much less thinking about one.

What she *did* need to think about was a job. Ideally, she wouldn't be here very long. But in the meantime, she had no income, dwindling savings, and a looming vet bill. And a potentially haunted house that might be difficult to sell.

So, she'd walked up and down Main Street, slightly amazed at the number of "Help Wanted" signs in windows. Tourist season, she surmised. She'd ended up applying for a hostess position at a restaurant and bar called The Boatyard and had been hired on the spot. Her training would be during the lunch shift in—she checked the clock—about nine hours. At some point, she'd need to get some more sleep, or she'd scare the customers.

A thread of anxiety thrummed through her veins as she studied her schedule. After everything she'd been through the last few nights, a new job shouldn't even faze her, but she didn't have any experience in the restaurant industry, unless you counted eating out. She'd studied business in school, at her father's urging, and most of her summer jobs had been at one of the Connecticut-area banks he managed. After graduation, she'd moved to New York City with her college roommate and eventually found an entry-level job at a prominent brokerage firm.

Then, after working her way up to broker's assistant, she was laid off unexpectedly as plans for a merger swirled. As was common in the business, she was given no warning, no time to possibly collect client information or sensitive material. Instead, she was quietly escorted out of the building after being given ten minutes to collect her personal items.

It hadn't even been the worst part of her day, as it turned out. But getting laid off like that had begun the downward spiral of her life that had landed her here. She gripped her mug, fighting to push the memories away. She couldn't bear to think about it right now.

Swigging the last of the milk, she stood and brought the mug to the sink. She used the bathroom, locked the back slider, and retrieved the poker from where it stood propped against the kitchen wall. Carrying it with her, she crossed into the living room and found her phone by the fireplace. She'd keep both things nearby—it was the best she could do.

God, she missed Preston. Just having another living being in the house had been comforting, even if he did spend most of the time beneath her bed. Hopefully he'd be ready to come home today, after her shift. She'd only have an hour window at that point to pick him up, but the vet's office wasn't far from The Boatyard.

The television here only received basic channels, but she found an old sit-com rerun to keep her company. No way was she spending the rest of the night in the room adjoining the study. She snapped open a blanket printed with seashells, giving silent thanks she'd had the foresight to wash it the other day as she inhaled the fresh scent. Then she settled in to spend yet another restless night on a couch.

5

*J*esse Holt said goodbye to his friends and left The Boatyard, which was still fairly crowded at 12:45 at night. Then again, it was a Friday in June, and The Boatyard was a favorite gathering spot for both locals and tourists, especially when there was live music, like tonight.

Straddling his bike, he strapped on his helmet and started the engine. He probably shouldn't have stayed so late, since he had to go into the office in the morning. One Saturday a month, he made sure he was available for clients who couldn't get in during the weekdays and needed appointments for issues beyond what the techs could handle.

Of course, the people in this town also knew he would be there in a heartbeat if there was an emergency. Even the new residents could easily find that out from his after-hours message. Lark Cavanaugh had.

A pulse of desire burned through him at the thought of the enticing redhead. Not only was she gorgeous, she was funny, even during as stressful a time as her cat's illness. Clearly, she loved animals, which was always a plus for him...in fact, she'd said something along the lines of her cat being all she had. What was that about? He recalled she'd said she had recently moved here, but he had no idea if she meant permanently or just for the summer. And his tech had filed Lark's paperwork before he had a chance to look at it.

Leaning into a turn, he left the streetlights of Main Street behind, slowing only slightly as his bike's headlamp became the only illumination in the otherwise unbroken darkness. But he knew these roads like the back of his hand, having spent most of his 29 years here. Hell, he'd even moved back into the house he'd been raised in after his father passed away and his mother decided to join some of her friends at an oceanfront retirement community. Financially, it had made a lot of sense, and since he'd promised his father he would keep the family business going—the vet office started by the elder Dr. Holt—it made sense in terms of location as well. In ten minutes, he could be at work...not a bad commute.

Cool wind whipped over his face, carrying the briny scent of saltwater and seaweed. Pine trees edged the road, their ranks parting only occasionally to reveal dirt lanes leading back into the woods. A few more turns and he was rumbling down his own driveway, a smile tugging on his lips as the silhouettes of his two dogs appeared in the window.

He parked in front of the garage and cut the engine, sweeping his gaze over the property. The house sat on nearly an acre, and much of the surrounding land remained undeveloped. Two-thirds of the entire town was protected from development as part of the Cape Cod National Seashore. While the population often swelled to 20,000 during the summer months, the year-round population hovered around 2,000 residents, making Truro the least populated town on Cape Cod. Sometimes the isolation came with an accompanying sense of loneliness, since it was just him and the dogs, but after some of the places he'd lived during his military duty, he usually appreciated the tranquility.

He knew Heather had been hoping they'd get back together when he finally returned home from Afghanistan after his final tour as an army vet. He'd served the required three years after being accepted into the Health Professions Scholarship Program and having his veterinary schooling paid for by the military. Heather Clancy, his on-again-off-again girlfriend since high school, had maintained contact throughout all the years he'd been in school and in the military, and while he appreciated the effort, he'd let her know—as gently as possible—that their last break-up really had been their last, that he didn't see a future for them together. He was sure in her mind, they'd only broken up because he'd left for his military tours, and when he came home last year to help his father, she'd still seemed to believe they'd find their way back to each other. While it was tempting sometimes, especially when the loneliness set in, he knew it wouldn't be fair to either one of them. He didn't love her. Not in the way he knew he'd need to in order to spend a life together. He'd seen deep, unconditional love in his parents' marriage. They'd truly enjoyed spending time together; they had still been best friends even after 34 years together. When his father passed away last fall, a part of his mother had died, too.

With a sigh, he removed his helmet and swung his leg off the bike. His more vocal dog, a pit bull mix named Bosco, was barking happily, while Benny, an older chocolate Lab, just wagged his tail in wild arcs, keeping his canine gaze on Jesse to make sure he continued on into the house.

A scream split the night, and Jesse froze, muscles tensing. *What the hell?* Instinctively, he reached for the 9mm he'd carried at all times overseas, but his hand came up empty. His own gun was locked in a safe in the house. He debated running into the house to retrieve it as both dogs barked frantically, their howls now ringing with alarm.

"Help! Help me!" The voice was female, high-pitched and filled with terror.

He hit the flashlight feature on his phone and took off, running around the garage toward the backyard. The cries seemed to be coming from somewhere behind his house, but he couldn't make out anyone in the open area of lawn leading down to the tree line.

A choked sob echoed from the dark woods at the bottom of the hill, and he speed up, his well-trained muscles quickly closing the distance. He vaguely remembered hearing the old woman who'd owned the property abutting his had passed away recently, and that relatives might be moving in. He wondered if he was about to get involved in a domestic dispute. Whatever was going on, a woman was clearly—and urgently—in distress, and he wasn't about to ignore her pleas for help in favor of waiting for the cops.

He slowed as he reached a large pine, pausing behind the thick trunk to scan the woods. He didn't want to barrel into a dangerous situation unprepared. On the other side of the river, something shifted in the shadows, and Jesse stilled, keeping his body hidden as he searched the darkness.

Across the river, a flash of white shimmered between the trees, catching the moonlight filtering through the canopy of branches. For a moment, he was thrust into the past, to the childhood nights he and his friends would hide in camouflaged forts, hoping for a glimpse of the fabled ghost of Holloway House. His mother claimed to have seen the phantom once, wandering along the edge of their yard. But he never had...up until now, anyway. *Could it be?*

A figure stumbled through the underbrush, coming into clear view. It was a flesh-and-blood woman, wearing a white shirt, and Jesse released a breath as his ridiculous thoughts of ghosts retreated to the realm of youthful imagination. But the woman *had* been calling for help, and now she flailed her arms as she staggered toward the river, as if fleeing an unseen attacker. With a guttural sob, she fell to her knees by the shallow bank.

He paused a beat, waiting for her pursuer to appear. But the woman was alone. Her pale skin glowed in the moonlight as she struggled against an invisible opponent. Goosebumps lifted the hairs on the back of his neck. What was going on here?

She collapsed, her dark hair falling forward as her chest hit the ground. "No, please," she moaned.

Sleepwalking? Night terrors? A psychotic break? He

snapped into action, running down the path toward the old wooden bridge. His footsteps pounded on the planks, the soft wood bending beneath his weight. The sound was thunderous in his ears, drowning out his heartbeat, but the woman didn't raise her head.

He reached her before she tumbled into the water, dropping to his knees and hauling her back. Icy air surrounded her, and he wondered if she was somehow suffering from hypothermia despite the warm night. She cried out again as she struggled against him, but as he turned her over, her eyes flew open and she stared up at him, blinking in confusion.

His breath caught. "Lark?"

"I…" Her vacant gaze began to sharpen as she fought to focus. "Dr. Holt? What's going on?" she asked, her brows pulling together. Leaves rustled beneath her hair as she turned her head to the sides, studying her surroundings. Fear still clouded her features, but distress seemed to be edging out sheer terror.

"I'm not sure," he answered gently, suddenly aware he was straddling her, his knees brushing against her hips. Probably not the most reassuring position for her to awaken to. And she was wearing very little—just the tiny T-shirt and underwear. But even being barely dressed didn't account for the chill he'd felt coming off of her. At least some of the color was returning to her face. "I think you were sleepwalking," he added as he eased off of her. "You were screaming for help."

"I was? I don't remember." She touched her forehead. "But I don't sleepwalk. Never in my life." Grimacing, she propped herself up on her elbows. As her gaze drifted down her body, a deeper flush darkened her cheeks. "Oh, God," she murmured under her breath.

He reached behind his neck and pulled off his own T-shirt. "Here. Put this on."

She didn't argue, just mechanically accepted the shirt and stared at it for a long moment as though it might hold the answers to how she came to be sitting in the woods, half-naked and woozy. Finally, she threaded her arms into it and slowly tugged it over her head. "Thank you."

Nodding, he stood up, offering her a hand. Warmth tingled through his palm as their skin connected, and he was relieved her body temperature was returning to normal. In the back of his mind, he was still debating calling 911, although now for an ambulance. He glanced over at his phone, lying in the dirt, the light still shining from the tiny bulb. "Are you hurt?" he asked, turning away to give her some privacy as she adjusted his shirt until it reached the middle of her thighs.

"No. I mean, I don't think so," she added, her voice still heavy with bewilderment.

"Why don't we go back to my house?" He jerked a thumb over his shoulder. "I live right up that hill."

"You…live there?" She peered past him, searching through the trees, then turned her head in the opposite direction, toward Holloway House.

"Yes. I think we're neighbors." He gave her a moment to process this.

"Oh." She hugged her arms across her chest. "Um, thanks, but I don't want to impose. Or disturb your family."

"It's just me." He dragged a hand through his hair. "Well, me and Bosco and Benny, my dogs."

Silence spooled out as a range of emotions flickered across her face. A shudder ran through her, and she exhaled audibly, casting a glance behind her. "I think...I think there's something wrong with that house."

"You wouldn't be the first person around here to say that," he said grimly. He fought the urge to touch her, gesturing with his hand instead. "Come on, let's get you warmed up. Get you something to drink."

He wasn't sure why he felt so strongly about her coming home with him, but he did, despite how much he'd been looking forward to getting to sleep less than thirty minutes ago. For some reason, an inexplicable urge to take care of her had taken over. The sudden need to protect her flowed through him, fierce and primal. And while he didn't really know if there was anything in that house she needed protection from, he wasn't lying about the rumors—people did say the place was cursed.

She nodded, silently turning toward the little bridge leading to his property.

As they crossed, he lost his internal battle and touched her upper arm. "Are you sure you're okay? I mean, physically?" He glanced down at her bare feet. "Your feet..."

"I think they're a little scratched up, but it's no big deal." She caught his gaze as he looked back up, a tight smile flickering across her lips. "Thanks for coming to my rescue. I'm... well, I'm mortified, actually. This is not exactly the first impression I wanted to make on my new neighbors." As she smoothed her hair, she picked out pieces of leaves and clumps of pine needles, dropping them back to the forest floor.

Their combined laughter eased some of the tension, and he was reminded again how she was able to find humor in awkward situations. It was a valuable trait, and one he found immensely appealing. "Well," he countered, cocking his head to the side. "To be fair, I think sleeping on my waiting room couch was really your first impression. Midnight sleepwalking through the woods just seems like the natural progression."

Her heavy sigh turned into a giggle she couldn't suppress. They crested the hill, and he led them toward the side of the house. "How's Preston doing?" he asked as he clicked his phone flashlight off.

"He's doing well so far. I set up all his stuff in the upstairs bathroom, and I keep him confined in there at night so he's right near his water and litter box. He seems content with that, actually. He doesn't like the house either." She blew out a breath. "I have to get us out of there."

"You're moving out, then?"

"Well, yes, as soon as I can sell the house. I want to get back to the city."

"Boston?"

"New York. That's where I've lived for the past three years. I grew up nearby, in Connecticut."

"Oh." An unexpected pang of disappointment tightened his chest. As they approached the house, Bosco and Benny appeared in the windows, their dual greeting of excited barking and joyful howls cutting off further conversation.

The dogs eagerly vied for Lark's attention as soon as they

got through the door, and Lark laughed, bending down to pet them. "They're so cute. What are their names again?"

"This one's Bosco," he said as he latched on to the dog's collar, hauling him back before he toppled Lark over. "Sorry, he loves new people. I've only had him for about six months. Someone found him on the side of the road and brought him in. He'd been hit by a car and no one ever claimed him."

"So you brought him home?" she finished, her green eyes shining with emotion. "That was so kind of you."

He shrugged. "He's a sweet dog. If a little overly enthusiastic." He released Bosco as she stood up. "And this is Benny. He's been our family dog for years." Scratching Benny behind one floppy brown ear, he added, "He sort of came with the house. When my dad passed away, my mom moved to a retirement community, and I moved back in here."

Her smile fell away as a cloud passed over her features. "I'm sorry."

"Thanks. He was a veterinarian too. He opened the clinic here 34 years ago."

"You must miss him."

"Yeah." Clearing his throat, he motioned for her to follow him into the living room. "Why don't you sit down? I'll get us something hot to drink. I have decaf and some of the tea my mom likes. Or something stronger if you'd like."

"Maybe just some warm milk, if you have it?" She tugged a hand through her auburn hair, grimacing when her fingers caught in the heavy waves. "I know that probably sounds juvenile, but..."

"It sounds perfect. Coming right up." He unfolded a blanket

as she sank onto the couch, spreading it over her. The dogs jumped up beside her and he sighed, shaking his head. "Sorry about that. We're lax on rules around here."

"It's fine," she said, tucking the blanket around herself with one hand as she tried to pet them both with the other. "It's nice company, actually."

He started to turn toward the kitchen, then realized he still wasn't wearing a shirt. As he switched directions, he caught her staring at his chest. She quickly looked away, her face coloring. Heat pulsed through his lower body, and he strode toward the staircase, calling out over his shoulder, "I'm just going to grab a shirt first. Be right back."

When he returned from the kitchen—wearing a shirt and carrying her drink—the dogs had settled down, one on either side of Lark. Her head was tipped back, eyes closed, but she opened them as he approached. He handed her the milk and sat down on the other end of the couch.

"Thanks, Dr. Holt," she murmured, lifting the mug to blow at the steam.

The corner of his mouth quirked up. "Under the circumstances, I think it's okay to call me Jesse."

Her lips curved into an answering smile as she sipped her drink. "Okay, thanks. I guess we are neighbors, after all."

He nodded, glancing out the front window into the darkness. "Do you want to talk about it? I mean, about what happened tonight?"

A deep sigh escaped as she stared down into her mug. "I do. It's just that I don't remember much. But other things have happened, before tonight, but I know it's going to sound ridiculous."

"Try me."

She chewed on her bottom lip, finally lifting her eyes to meet his gaze. "Well, when I first arrived, I thought I saw a face in one of the upstairs windows. Then there's the noises...I've been woken up by loud thumping and something that sounds like moaning a few nights now, including the night I found Preston so sick. A picture fell off the wall. And now this." She hiked one shoulder in a small shrug. "All I can remember is a feeling of being chased. The need to get away, to get help. And when you woke me up..." she drifted off, a slight flush returning to her cheeks. "This is going to sound crazy. But when you first found me, as I was waking up or whatever, my head felt... crowded. Like I was fighting for control or something."

"It doesn't sound crazy. That's what it looked like. You fell down as though you were pushed. And then, when I grabbed you, it was because you looked like you were about to fall into the river."

The pink hue of her skin turned a shade darker, and she looked down, plucking at the blanket on her lap. "Well, I suppose that would have woken me up," she said, her voice threaded with forced lightheartedness.

"I hope so. I'm just glad you're not hurt."

"Yeah, me too. And I'm sorry if I freaked you out."

"Don't apologize. The whole thing must have been terrifying," he said gently, searching for the right words to ease her embarrassment. "Listen, Lark...I believe you." That felt right, and it was true, for the most part. Whether he could bring himself to believe in ghosts was one thing, but he did believe she'd heard strange noises and had a frightening sleepwalking episode. "My mother thought she saw something down near the woods, once. She was convinced it was a ghost."

"Really?"

His heart twisted at the gratitude playing across her face. "Yes. And I wasn't exaggerating about the rumors...lots of people around here do think that house is...well, haunted."

"I did know about that before I moved in...it's just that, well, I didn't have a lot of choices. And I didn't believe in ghosts, either. But now, I'm starting to second-guess that." A tremor ran through her, and she tightened both hands around the mug.

"What exactly were you told about the house?"

She finished her drink, leaning forward to set the mug down on the coffee table. Bosco put his paw on her lap, and she settled a hand on his wide head. "Not a lot, really. I should probably know more about it, but it was a weird set of circumstances. And everything happened so quickly. I found out I inherited this house, and then suddenly I needed a place to stay. I had nowhere else to go, so I just decided it was fate."

Another reference to not having anyone else she could depend on in her life. He wanted to ask her about it, but this was not the time. "Makes sense."

"All I really know is that the house belonged to relatives on my mother's side of the family, and that when my great aunt Joan died, she left it to me. Oh, and that people here think it's haunted because two people died there." She grimaced, the faint freckles on the bridge of her nose bunching together. "I guess I should do a little research on that. My understanding was that there was an accident and a suicide."

He dragged a hand along his jaw, the stubble reminding him it was now the middle of the night. He really did need to get to sleep, since he had to work in the morning. And yet, as tired as he'd been an hour ago, now he only wanted to keep talking to Lark. But he should really encourage her to get some rest, too. In the bright light of the living room, he couldn't help noticing the violet smudges shadowing her eyes.

His mind went rogue for a moment, picturing him bringing her upstairs and into his bed. Wrapping his arms around her, kissing her tenderly…

God, he was awful. He pushed the inappropriate image from his thoughts, struggling to focus on the conversation. The very serious conversation that should not lend itself at all to sexual fantasies, no matter how much chemistry he felt between them. That was probably all in his head as well.

"What do *you* know about the house?" she asked after a few beats of silence.

"Not much more than that. What I've heard is a local pastor and his wife lived there in the 1950s, and she fell down the stairs and broke her neck. Some years after that, the husband committed suicide. Hung himself." He grimaced, rubbing his knuckles. "Various stories have taken hold since then. I've heard things like maybe it wasn't an accident, and she's haunting the place because he killed her. Or maybe it *was* an accident, but she wanted him to join her, and her ghost was trying to drive him to suicide. Or that he went crazy with grief and loneliness and tried to end it by killing himself, but all the negative energy remained, along with his spirit." He shrugged. "Those are the things I heard growing up, anyway. And then some people just say the house is cursed, and it's both of them haunting the place."

She scrunched up the side of her mouth. "Great."

"Yeah. Again, those are the rumors. But if you want, I can ask my mother. She'd know more, especially having lived here so long. And her friends might know more details too."

"Okay, thanks. I don't know if it will help, but at the very least, I should probably know that part of my family history." Raising her hand, she stifled a yawn.

"You must be tired. Do you want to sleep here?"

Color rose in her cheeks again, and he realized how his offer must sound. "I mean, in one of the guest rooms," he added hurriedly. "Or, you know, on the couch." A grin twitched at the corners of his lips.

She chuckled wearily. "Thank you, but I should get home. Besides, I prefer to sleep on much smaller couches, especially in public places if possible."

"You sure?" *I'd feel much better if you were here.* But he quickly realized *she* probably wouldn't. She barely even knew him. Why would she feel safe alone in an isolated house with a man who was virtually a stranger?

She nodded, shifting forward and extricating herself from between the two dogs. Benny opened one eye and made a noise somewhere between a grunt and a sigh. "I should get home and shower. I need to get cleaned up, and I want to check on Preston."

"Here, take the blanket," he instructed as she stood up. Before she could protest, he draped it around her shoulders. His brow wrinkled as he glanced at her lower body. Angry red scratches marred the smooth skin of her legs, and the bottoms of her feet were probably equally torn up. "You want to borrow some shoes? Or socks, at least?"

"Thanks, but I'm fine. I'll stick to the path this time." She curled her fingers around the edges of the blanket and gathered it around her chest like a shawl.

"I'll walk you home."

"That's not necessary, really. I've taken enough of your time."

He hoped her concern truly was more about inconveniencing him rather than not feeling safe with him, because on this matter, he was not going to budge. "I'll walk you home. It's safe around here for the most part, but still…I need to know you get back okay."

She nodded. "Okay, thanks."

At the word "walk", both dogs had pricked their ears, and tags jingled as they jumped off the couch and looked at the door hopefully.

He rolled his eyes as she laughed. "Fine, you guys can come too." Grabbing his phone, he opened the door and let them all out into the night.

"They don't need leashes?" she asked as the dogs bounded ahead of them toward the backyard.

"No, they're pretty good about listening. Well, Benny is, and Bosco will usually follow Benny."

"I'd love to have a dog someday. It's hard in the city, though."

There it was again. He hesitated, then dove in. "Is there someone…special…waiting for you there? Boyfriend?"

She gave a harsh laugh. "No, definitely not. No boyfriend, waiting or otherwise."

A surge of relief flowed through him. He'd suspected as much, after what she'd said about not having anyone that night at his office, but it was good to have confirmation. Although he wasn't sure it made a difference. What was he going to do…try to start a relationship with her when he knew she was desperate to leave?

An awkward silence began to unspool, and he cast about for something to fill it. "But your family lives there?"

An insect jumped away from their footsteps with a loud buzz of protest. "No," she said, her voice slow and heavy. "My family is gone. My parents passed away, and I'm an only child."

Crap. He clenched his jaw, closing his eyes for a moment. "I'm really sorry, Lark." As they entered the woods between their houses, the dogs came flying from the side of the yard to join them.

"It's okay." She adjusted the blanket, hunching her shoulders and pulling it tighter. "Honestly, there's nothing waiting for me in New York. Not even a job or an apartment, at this point. It's just…what I'm used to. I grew up going into the city for dinners and events. I went to college there, and then I lived there for three years after school. There are so many cool places…there's always something to do." Clearing her throat, she shrugged inside her blanket. "It's home, you know?"

"I do know," he said as they crossed the bridge. Beneath their feet, the river ran sluggishly along its course to the ocean. Something slipped into the water, the small splash catching the dogs' attention. "No! Don't go in," he commanded in an authoritative tone.

"Have you always lived here?" she asked, picking her way around a shallow ditch along the trail.

"Well, I grew up here. My mom's family was from here, and when my parents married, they decided to settle down here, and my father opened the vet clinic. But I went to college in California."

"Wow…that's a long way from Cape Cod."

"Well, my older brother, Ryan, went to school on the west coast, so I had visited a few times. He still lives there. I came back east for veterinary school, and got accepted into a military program called HPSP. Health Professionals Scholarship Program. Basically, the army paid for my grad school, and I served as a military vet for three years. So I moved around quite a bit during active duty."

She slowed, turning to look at him. "Whoa. Did you live overseas?"

"For my second tour, yes. I was in Afghanistan."

"Jeez. That must have been scary. You must be glad to be back here."

"I am. I mean, it is awfully quiet here sometimes in the off season, but after a war zone, there's something to be said for the peacefulness."

As if on cue, a breeze rustled the branches overhead. Through chinks in the forest canopy, stars blazed with fiery brilliance, their luster intensified in the absence of manmade lights.

Lark murmured a small sound of agreement. "It *is* peaceful." She glanced up the hill as they came to the edge of her yard. "I just wish I didn't live in a haunted house."

"Yeah, it's less than ideal." They chuckled together, and he added, "The offer stands, by the way...if you ever need a different place to stay, I have room."

"Thanks."

He sensed her guard going up again, which seemed to happen any time he offered her help. What had happened in her past to make her so wary? She seemed afraid to appear vulnerable—even more afraid than of sleeping in a house she felt was haunted.

Maybe she just didn't want *his* help. Maybe the chemistry he felt sparking between them was completely one-sided. And if he was imagining romantic connections, it was probably time to get back to dating. He'd had a brief relationship with a grad student spending the summer here when he'd returned stateside last year, but she returned to her studies around the same time his father suddenly passed away, and there just wasn't enough holding them together to keep it going. Autumn and winter had been a whirlwind of grief and planning as he took over running the clinic and helped his mother move. He hadn't had the time or interest in dating, despite Heather's attempts to insinuate herself into his life again during the fallout of his family's loss.

He sighed inwardly. That wasn't fair. Maybe he was being too cynical. Heather wasn't a bad person—he wouldn't have dated her for three years if she was. It was just that she was used to getting what she wanted, and she seemed to have *him* in her sights. She'd brought over prepared meals from her family's market long after other friends had stopped…but she'd also used every visit to get close to him physically, forcing him to summon the strength to resist her while remaining polite. It was flattering—and sometimes tempting—but mostly just exhausting.

"Have you always wanted to be a vet?" she asked, dragging him from his dark thoughts.

He rubbed the back of his neck. "Yes. I loved watching my father work, loved helping him at the clinic when I got older. I did my undergrad in three years so I could move on to vet school faster."

"That must have been nice."

"What, finishing undergrad in three years?"

"No, knowing what you wanted to do with your life. Having a passion that's also a career."

"It's been good," he agreed, shortening his stride to keep pace with her as they climbed the sloping hill. "What do you do?"

"I studied business in college, mostly because my dad insisted that was the practical thing to do. So I ended up with a job at a brokerage firm, but I got laid off." She hesitated, as though she were about to say more.

"I'm sorry. That sucks."

"Yeah. It happened literally a week after I inherited this house, so coming here seemed like a good option to regroup."

Bosco raced by, eager to investigate a new place. Benny

loped along a few moments later and slowed to walk beside them. "And you're hoping to sell the house?"

"That's the plan. I need the money, frankly. I think I'm going to need to make some upgrades, though, and I'm not sure how I'm going to afford that. There's a trust attached to the house that was meant for upkeep, so I need to check with the lawyer to see if I can access that. I don't think there's much left, though." She sighed. "And I suppose I need to get rid of the ghost, too."

He called Bosco back as they rounded the side of the house. The outdoor lights glowed from the porch, and the front door stood wide open to the night. Moths swirled around the bright beacons in an excited cloud of activity.

"Great. I guess I forgot to close the door when I took my midnight stroll."

"You want me to check the house?" he asked, climbing the porch steps behind her. Before the dogs could barrel into her house, he commanded them to sit and stay.

She peered inside, then turned back to him. "No, that's okay. But thanks. For everything."

He didn't want the conversation to end. He still wanted to know what *her* passion was. What her childhood had been like, and what had happened to her family. Why she seemed determined not to accept his help. What made her happy and what made her sad. Her favorite food. Hell, he wanted to know all about her. But it was late, and they both needed sleep. And she was standing by the open door, wrapped in a blanket, waiting for him to leave.

"You're welcome. You still have my cell number if you need

me, right? Just call if something weird happens. I leave it on all night, and I can be here in five minutes."

Her eyes glistened with moisture, and she looked away, fighting back tears. "Thank you," she said again, her voice breaking slightly.

His heart contracted. "Really, it's no problem."

She swallowed hard, meeting his gaze again. "Would you really ask your mom for information about the house? I think I need to know what happened here. I'm going to do some research tomorrow, but..." she trailed off, shrugging a shoulder.

"Of course. I'll be at the clinic, but I'll give her a call when I have a break. My mom would love a project like this. She'll have all her friends in the retirement community gathering intel."

Emotions played across her face, and then suddenly she was hugging him, her arms wrapped around his neck. He instinctively embraced her, pulling her closer as his stunned mind fought to catch up. The blanket had puddled to the floorboards of the porch, and his hands slid in soothing circles over her back. Beneath the layers of their combined shirts, her flesh trembled slightly.

"Thank you. For everything," she whispered. "I know I keep repeating myself."

"It's fine. If you need help, I'm here." Bosco pressed against their legs, desperate to share the affection.

She loosened her grip, and he released her, inhaling her scent as they stepped apart. Citrus, sleep, and the woods. Reaching out, he pulled a pine needle from her hair.

"Get some rest," he instructed as she bent to pick up the blanket. "And stay in bed this time."

"I'll try." She gave him a wan smile as she held the blanket out to him. "You get some rest, too."

They locked eyes for a moment, the air between them growing still and heavy, as though an electrical storm was gathering strength to break open the sky. She turned away, stepping toward the open door, and the moment passed.

"Night, Lark."

"Goodnight, Doc—" She cut herself off and started again. "Jesse."

6

The boxes she'd brought from New York were still in the dining room, stacked against the wall. No need to unpack the personal items she wouldn't use on a daily basis —it would just be that much more work when she was ready to leave. She hadn't had time to label anything before she fled from the apartment, so she hefted the first one from the floor and set it on the long table. Chewing on her lip, she lifted the flaps cautiously, as though a creepy puppet on a spring might pop out.

No jack-in-the-box surprise greeted her, and she exhaled. God, living in this house was really getting to her. She glanced at the jagged scratch on her arm from last night's sleepwalking incident. At least she'd fallen back asleep—and stayed asleep— until the morning. But it had been another night spent on a couch.

After Jesse had left, she'd joined Preston in the bathroom, giving the snoozing cat some head scratches before taking a quick shower and then disinfecting the cuts on her skin. As she'd run a comb through her wet hair, she'd flicked her gaze between her steamy reflection and the borrowed shirt lying beside the sink. Eventually, she'd lost her internal debate and pulled Jesse's T-shirt back over her head before going downstairs for the remainder of the night. It made her feel more secure—what was the harm in that? A stern inner voice had quickly begun listing the potential harm, but she'd shut it out. She needed rest, and she'd use whatever means necessary to get it.

Of course, there was no explanation for why she was still wearing it now. Sighing, she bent forward and pulled a few file folders out of the box.

Her gaze fell on a black strap, and she sucked in a breath. Her camera case. Grief clamped around her heart like the steel jaws of a trap as she lifted it out with trembling fingers.

Photography had been her mother's passion, and when Lark began taking an interest, Carol Cavanaugh had been thrilled to share her knowledge. Over the years, they'd spent countless hours together scouting locations and capturing images, usually relying on nature for inspiration. They'd frame their favorites, giving them as gifts or selling them at craft fairs. Lark even won a contest once with a photo of the sun setting over Silver Lake.

She'd received this camera for her 21st birthday, as a replacement for the hand-me-down of her mother's she'd been using. She'd been working on a series of photos set in Central Park, a theme of the four seasons, when her parents died. She'd never finished the winter shots. After the crash, she'd put the camera away.

Cradling the case to her chest, she glanced across the dining room and beyond the slider, to the sunlit backyard. Maybe it was time to start taking pictures again. There were so many beautiful places here. And her friend Madison had insisted many artists and photographers come to Cape Cod just for the spectacular light.

Two tiny sparrows flitted around the inexpensive birdfeeder she'd set up, finally landing on the thin rail around the seed tray. Preston's tail twitched as he watched from his new cat perch. That hadn't been inexpensive, but she'd decided he needed a spot of his own—somewhere he'd feel safe—if she was ever going to get him downstairs. So she'd headed to Wellfleet to find a pet store, and come home with both the cat tower and the bird feeder—entertainment she knew he wouldn't be able to resist. She had to admit, she was enjoying watching all the different species suddenly coming to visit. Even the squirrels were cute, if exasperating. Despite the seed she scattered on the ground, they still seemed determined to get to the hanging food.

Nodding to herself, she gently placed the camera down on the table. She could start taking pictures of the birds, maybe. Slowly get back into it. Her mom would like that. When her parents had been planning their anniversary trip to Hawaii, her mother couldn't stop talking about all the beautiful locations and breathtaking vistas she was hoping to photograph.

A fresh spike of pain lanced through her, and she turned her attention back to the contents of the box. Right now, she had a different project she needed to focus on. After digging through the remainder of the items in the first box, she put everything but the camera back and then exchanged it for the next.

Bingo. This one held what she was looking for: her baby book. As difficult as it was to even look at the pink cover of the collection of memories, she knew there was a family tree inside that might help her piece together the history of this house. Steeling herself, she carried it into the kitchen, pausing on the way to stroke Preston's back.

She placed the baby book on the kitchen table, beside her laptop, which was open to the email folder containing the correspondence about the house. A warm breeze drifted through the open window above the sink as she rinsed out her coffee cup, and she breathed in the scent of pine needles and ocean air. Then she poured the rest of this morning's coffee into her mug and heated it up. She'd probably had enough caffeine already today, but she felt like she needed something stronger than water for the task at hand, and it was too early for wine. Not to mention she had to be at work when the lunch shift began at 11:00.

By the time the last sips of her coffee had grown cold, she'd come up with a timeline that, while not offering any glaring revelations, at least gave her a clear idea of who this house had belonged to and how it had ended up in her possession. When John died, the house went to Martha's older sister, Elizabeth. From there it passed down to Elizabeth's oldest daughter, Joan. Sadly, Joan's only child died as a teenager, but Joan lived until the age of 90, spending some of her last years in Holloway

House before moving to a nursing home. Joan's younger sister had been Lark's grandmother—her mother's mother. Which technically made Joan her grand aunt, although most people just used the term great aunt. An online search of the specific family names didn't produce much more than basic dates and obituaries.

She tapped her pen against her chart. What did she have for clues so far, in terms of who might be haunting this house? A figure in the spare bedroom window. Bumps in the night, moans and cold air. A picture falling off the wall. Sleepwalking in the night and nearly falling into the river in a trance.

Scrunching her mouth, she sat back in the chair. Honestly, all those things could be chalked up to imagination mixed with events that had reasonable, completely normal explanations. Sure, she'd never heard nonexistent voices or had night terrors before, but she was in an entirely new environment, not to mention still reeling from the upheaval of her former life. The change and stress could be causing unusual actions and perceptions.

But...the rumors. And the figure Jesse's mother had seen. Perhaps it was all just the power of suggestion stemming from the combination of an abandoned house with a tragic history and a need for drama in a quiet town.

She glanced over at Preston, his muscles tense as he tracked the birds from behind the glass. The cat had certainly seemed uncomfortable in this house. But then again, maybe he was just picking up on her emotions. "Maybe there's no haunting here at all, Pres," she murmured in his direction. "No ghosts."

A sharp thud cracked above her head, and she screamed,

launching herself out of the chair. It toppled backwards as she scanned the ceiling, her hand clutching her chest as though she might be able to control her wildly clattering heart from the outside. From the corner of her eye she saw Preston bolt around the corner, a blurry streak of gray and white. She slowly backed into the counter, her fingers gripping the edge as she waited for something else to happen.

No sound followed beyond the rush of blood in her ears, and as her breathing slowed, she made her way back to the table on wobbly legs. Righting the chair, she leaned on the back for a moment. *It's okay.* Something just fell again, like the picture. Her gaze drifted to the family tree she'd been working on. The timing seemed a little too convenient—she suggests, out loud, that there's no ghosts here, and the answer is a loud bang from upstairs? With a sigh, she pushed herself away from the chair and trudged up the back stairs to go investigate.

Upstairs, the bathroom and its adjoining walls were above the area where the kitchen table sat, so she surveyed the bathroom first. Nothing seemed amiss, which didn't surprise her. Every cell in her body relayed the same message—the sound had come from the study off the master bedroom. The wall where the fallen picture had hung was on the other side of the bathroom. She'd left the pastor's portrait on the floor, but perhaps the matching portrait of his wife had tumbled down to reunite with its mate. A shudder ran through her as she made her way toward the study door.

A tendril of icy air snaked around her, as though trying to pull her forward. She resisted, latching on to the door frame to steady herself. Goosebumps lifted the hairs on the back of her neck as her gaze darted to the left wall. The lone portrait remained on the wall. But the large wooden cross that had hung above the portraits was now on the floor.

Oh, God. Her vision swam, nausea churning in her belly like curdled milk. Why was this happening? And what was it supposed to mean?

Maybe it's just something inside the wall causing things to fall, a desperate inner voice insisted. A vibration from the pipes.

She shoved the pleas for rational explanations aside. The timing was just too suspicious. Still clutching the wall, she scanned the nearby bookshelves for clues. If a ghost *was* trying to tell her something, what was the message?

One of the framed pictures on the shelf caught her attention: an old photo of the town church. The white steeple rose into a cloudless sky, and trees and gravestones surrounded the simple wooden chapel. Her gaze slid from the graveyard in the picture to the Bible shelved beside it, and something in her mind clicked.

John had been the pastor of that parish—a pillar of the community, a religious leader. After losing his wife, and then his mind, he'd taken his own life. Wasn't that considered a sin in most Christian religions, especially back then? Maybe he hadn't been buried with the regular service because of that. Sunday school hadn't exactly been a big part of her childhood, but it sounded plausible. And something like that might prevent a regular person's spirit from resting in peace, never mind someone who had dedicated their life to God. If John was the ghost, maybe that's what he needed—forgiveness for committing suicide. A full Christian burial, whatever that entailed.

"Is that it?" she whispered into the study, her voice a hoarse croak. She cleared her throat. "Pastor John can't rest in peace until he has a proper service?"

Rubbing her palms along her arms, she waited for some kind of response. When nothing happened, she lifted a shoulder. It couldn't be *that* easy for a ghost to communicate, right? Otherwise, it would just tell her what the hell it wanted and be done with it. There'd be no need for these games and clues.

She had to have figured it out correctly! The portrait, the cross, even the nightmare that brought her outdoors, calling for help and collapsing to the ground—it all fit. Excitement bubbled through her as she dropped onto her bed and grabbed her cell off the nightstand. She needed to tell Jesse the news. Bouncing her leg, she scrolled through her screen to find his number.

Wait. Jesse had said he had to work today. Maybe she should text him instead of calling...

Her thumbs flew over the keypad for a few seconds before she caught herself. *What on earth am I doing?* Jesse was not her partner in this. Why was her first reaction to talk to him about this anyway? She needed to be more careful. He wasn't her friend, he was her neighbor. And her cat's vet.

She needed to rein in the feelings she was developing for him. Immediately. Whether she could stop her body's physical reaction to him was another matter, though. God, he was just so hot. The image of his shirtless torso flashed in her mind—

hard planes, taut muscles, wide shoulders. Strong arms she wanted to feel wrapped around her...

No. She pushed the thoughts away, ignoring the warmth tingling low in her belly. She couldn't risk her heart again. Ever. The only person she could trust was herself. The past few weeks had taught her it was best to keep everyone else at a safe distance.

Then again, sex didn't have to involve emotions. Lots of people had one night stands and never saw the person again. Sex could just be about the physical pleasure. Her memory pulled up Jesse again, his handsome face so close to hers in the soft glow of the porch lights.

She laughed out loud. What was she thinking? What made her imagine for even one hot second Jesse was interested in sleeping with her? That man could have anyone he wanted. He wouldn't choose the crazy lady next door who slept on his office couch and ran through the woods at night screaming. The woman who literally no one cared about. The friend and fiancé who mattered so little that hurting her—betraying her— was both easy and enjoyable.

Swallowing down the self-pity, she pushed herself off the bed. Her legs felt heavy as she trudged back down the stairs, but she tried to remind herself she now had a theory. She wasn't exactly sure how to proceed from here, but still...it was something. She searched around for Preston, eventually locating him beneath the couch, where he seemed determined to stay. With a small shake of her head, she folded the blanket on what was apparently her new bed. A twinge traveled through her lower back as she straightened, and she considered heading out back to the porch to do some stretching. Sleeping on the couch might be better for her mentally, but physically, it wasn't doing her body any favors.

She crossed into the kitchen to check the time, grimacing when she realized she had less than an hour to get ready and get to The Boatyard. With a soft sigh, she closed her baby book and picked it up. Cradling it against her chest, she carried it through the dining room and settled it back into its box. The camera still sat on the table, and her gaze lingered on it for a moment before she turned away and headed for the stairs. There was a storm predicted this evening. Maybe later she would try to capture some shots as it rolled in across the Atlantic.

7

A light tap on the door of his office pulled his attention from the computer screen on his desk. "Come in," he called as he set his sandwich down beside the keyboard.

Diane peeked in, her pewter hair floating around her head. "You have a visitor."

His mind jumped to Lark. *Was she okay?* He'd been thinking of her all morning, debating whether to text her. He'd gone as far as locating her initial call to him and making her a contact in his phone.

"Heather's out front," Diane finished, her lips pursing around the statement. The sour note of distaste was now apparent in her tone. Diane was the maternal figure in the office, and she wasn't a fan of Heather.

The unexpected buoyancy in his chest deflated, leaving only continued concern for Lark mixed with a new thread of tension. He'd gotten little sleep, he was busy, and he wasn't in the mood to deal with any of Heather's drama.

"I told her you were having a working lunch, but you know..." She let the unfinished sentence hang in the air, her shoulder lifting in a shrug.

He did know. Heather had never been one to take "no" easily. He thought he'd been pretty clear about the fact that he didn't see a future for them as a couple, but now he had a feeling she thought he was just playing hard to get. He frowned. If she knew him as well as she thought she did, she'd understand games weren't his thing.

Sighing, he took a swig from his water bottle. "I do know," he responded.

"Do you want me to tell her you said to take a hike?" A hopeful glimmer shone in her hazel eyes.

He gave a grim laugh. "No, then she'll just think it's coming from you. But thanks." He pushed his wheeled chair back and stood. "I'll go see what she wants."

"She brought food. I tried to get her to just give it to me, but she wasn't interested in just dropping it off." Diane's nose wrinkled.

"It's fine."

Diane nodded and opened the door wider for him before she headed back toward the front desk. He pushed a hand through his hair as he followed her.

Heather was at the far end of the desk, tapping away at her phone, a bag and two iced coffees sitting in front of her. She looked up as he approached, a bright smile flashing across her tanned face. She stuck her phone in the back pocket of minis-cule jeans shorts and tossed her blonde hair back. "Hey, Jess. Mom made a huge batch of cranberry muffins this morning, and I know how much you love them, so I brought you some." She gestured perfectly manicured hands toward the white bakery bag with "Clancy's Market" printed on the front.

Heather's family had owned Clancy's for as long as he could remember, and Heather worked at the upscale market and bakery as well. The prices were high, but the shop drew all the summer tourists, as well as a group of loyal year-round residents. Plus, it was the only place to find groceries in Truro, so Clancy's benefited from shoppers who needed to pick up a few items and didn't have time to make a longer trip.

"Thanks."

She beamed at him again. "Sure. And some fresh iced coffee." She reached for one of the clear plastic cups and closed her lips around the straw. Glancing out the windows as she sipped, she added, "It's supposed to storm later, but it's beautiful out now. Why don't you take a break? We can go sit outside and enjoy the sun."

He caught Diane's frown in his peripheral vision as disapproval rolled off of her like laser beams. He couldn't help but slide the iced coffee toward him, though. He needed a healthy dose of caffeine, and Clancy's did make a great cold brew. "I can't right now, I have a lot of work to catch up on. But tell your mom thanks for the muffins. And the coffee." He took a quick pull, savoring the smooth, strong flavor.

Her mouth curved into a pout as she exhaled a disappointed sigh. "Okay." She titled her head, her brown eyes honing in on his. "Hey, did you hear Russell is coming home for the weekend?"

Rubbing the back of his neck, he nodded. Russell Kuhn was

another old friend from high school. He'd heard something about his visit the other night at The Boatyard. "I did hear that."

"Everyone's getting together at The Boatyard on Friday night. You're in, right?"

"I should be able to make it," he hedged. He was planning on it, but he tried to choose his words carefully around Heather these days. If he gave her any leeway, she might try to turn his response into a commitment to her rather than an opportunity to see his buddies.

"Great," she said enthusiastically, totally dismissing his indecisiveness. "What else have you got going on this weekend?"

He glanced pointedly at the clock on the far wall. "Um…just a lot of work."

She bounced her chin in a nod, either missing or ignoring his unspoken signals. "I'm having dinner with my parents tomorrow night for their anniversary."

"Ah. Tell them happy anniversary for me."

"I will. How's your mom doing?"

"Good." He didn't offer the fact that he was having dinner with her tomorrow night as well. It would be just like Heather to try to combine the family dinners into one big group event. He made a mental note to pick a restaurant the Clancys would be unlikely to choose.

Her eyes narrowed as she finally accepted he wasn't going to do his part to prolong the conversation. "That's good." She plucked sunglass off the top of her head. "Well, I'll let you get back to it, then. Stop by the store if you need more. Of anything," she added, tipping her chin toward the bakery bag.

God, he hoped that last phrase didn't have the double meaning he was hearing. With a curt nod, he stepped back from the desk. "Thanks again."

"Anytime. See you Friday," she sang out over her shoulder as she sauntered through the waiting room and out into the sunshine.

8

---

*a*s forecasted, dark clouds were already gathering on the horizon when Lark returned home from work. She glanced up as she strode toward the house, trying to judge how much time she had. Overhead, the sky remained a pale blue, the afternoon sun still emitting a soft glow that warmed her skin. If she hurried, she could probably get some great pictures of the oncoming storm, and maybe even some shots of lightening over the water, before the predicted rain made its way to the beach.

For some reason, the idea of taking photographs again had her excited. She hadn't touched her camera in nearly two years, except to store it in that box, but now, using it again almost felt like a compulsion. One that made her slightly giddy. It felt like a positive sign, and she smiled at it as she made her way through the dining room to the kitchen. She wanted to grab a quick snack before she left.

Preston wasn't sitting on his cat tower, she noted as she

passed the slider. Hopefully he had headed upstairs to his bed in the bathroom and wasn't still under the couch. She had to get rid of this ghost, not just for her own sanity and the sale of the house, but for Preston's well-being too.

Biting into an apple, she glanced at her notes on the little kitchen table. A frown pulled at her mouth as she noticed a brown stain marring the top of her carefully-drawn family tree. Her coffee mug had tipped over, spilling liquid across some of the names. She took a step closer, her hand holding the apple falling to her side. The blurred names were at the head of the tree: John and Martha.

A shiver scurried up her spine. She'd jumped when the cross upstairs had fallen...she'd moved so quickly, the chair had toppled. But she was almost positive she hadn't knocked her coffee mug over. Another message? Or just something she hadn't noticed earlier, in the commotion from the fallen cross and her excitement over her theory?

Her theory. If it was correct, something could be done to possibly end this. She flicked her gaze between the window over the sink and the laptop on the table. It wouldn't take long to Google a few things.

Twenty minutes later, she was ready to leave the house, after locating Preston in the bathroom, changing into a navy T-shirt dress, and packing a duffle bag with her camera and a raincoat, just in case. The walk to the beach was a good 15 minutes, but she felt like getting the exercise. She wouldn't melt if she got wet. And the camera would be protected in its case inside the duffle bag. If it was really pouring, she could wrap it in the plastic bags she'd brought along as well.

As she descended the porch steps, she paused, inhaling the clean air touched with the scent of impending rain. She had to admit, if it wasn't for the haunting, this house—and this town—had its charm. The changing light bathed the surrounding trees in a golden glow and gilded the clouds with radiant halos.

Fishing out her camera, she made a few adjustments, then walked backwards to frame the house through the viewfinder. Her finger hovered over the button for a moment as she drew in a shaky breath. Then she depressed the button, releasing the shutter, a similar feeling of release surging through her with the soft click. There. She'd done it. She was taking photos again.

She walked around the house, capturing images of the woods and the river. Maybe she'd send a few to Madison. While they weren't as close as they used to be, when they'd worked together at the brokerage firm before Madison left for a different position, Madison had been a true friend during that last difficult week in New York. She'd allowed Lark to sleep on her couch, despite the desperately cramped confines of her tiny apartment. She'd facilitated the use of the borrowed car from a co-worker spending a month in China—a guy Lark had never even met. A pang of gratitude tightened her chest as she packed the camera back up. There *were* kind people in the world. She would get them both gift cards to thank them, once her financial situation was on steadier ground. And if her pictures came out well, maybe she'd also matte and frame one for each of them.

The walk felt good—walking was something she did so much in the city as part of her regular routine, she'd forgotten she would need to make time for it here. And she'd been learning about the various trails she needed to visit from some of her new coworkers. Many of the wait staff were Eastern European, here for the summer on work visas, and they spent most of their free time touring the local landmarks and scenic sites. She needed to do a better job of that, as long as she was here. She'd take her camera along, too.

She'd seen this part of the Cape Cod National Seashore already, on one of her initial drives around town, but it still took her breath away. In fact, the climb up the hill to reach the steep cliffs guarding the beach below almost literally took her breath away. Yep, she really needed to get back into a cardio routine. At least she'd been keeping up with her yoga practice. It not only kept her muscles strong, it unlocked the cramped knots and eased the constant tension. But she would have to start walking and jogging again soon. There was no excuse... she wouldn't even have to get herself over to Central Park for a long run. This whole town was like one big park.

Once she reached the top of the hill, she spent a few moments taking in the majestic sand dunes, the miles of beach stretching in either direction, and the endless expanse of ocean reaching out to meet the sky on the distant horizon. Despite the oncoming storm, a few tenacious beachgoers still dotted the landscape, but they were few and far between.

She kicked off her flip-flops, shouldered the duffel bag, and took a few photos from her vantage point. Then she made her way down the switchback path cutting through the high, sheer dunes toward the beach.

The sand beneath her feet still held on to the day's warmth, but the approaching clouds were turning the sky leaden. In the distance, a mass of thunderheads formed a menacing black smudge.

She stopped at a spot midway to the surf and snapped another series of photos. Then she unfurled the blanket she'd stowed in her bag and sat down to watch the changing weather and the strengthening waves. A trio of seagulls stood by the edge of the water, the rising wind buffeting their gray and white feathers. The strands of hair that had escaped her topknot fluttered around her face, and she tucked them back behind her ears.

She felt the vibration beneath the sand seconds before she sensed the rapid movement behind her. She twisted around just in time to see a flash of black and white barreling toward her before the solid weight of a large dog was nearly in her lap.

"Bosco!" a deep voice called. "Come!"

Her muscles relaxed as she realized she knew her unexpected canine visitor. "Hi, boy," she said, giggling as he whined with excitement and butted his large head into her chest. Rubbing his smooth fur, she searched the beach, her gaze quickly landing on Jesse's tall form as he made his way down the dunes, Benny at his heels. Her heart did a little flip, and she gave herself a mental kick. *Stop.*

Jesse jogged across the sand toward her, Benny loping alongside. "Sorry," he called as he approached her. Benny finally cut ranks and raced ahead to join Bosco on her blanket, leaving Jesse to give them both a disapproving scowl when he arrived. But a smile took its place as he greeted her. "Hey, Lark. Sorry about that."

"It's fine, really," she assured him, trying to pet both dogs simultaneously as they wiggled around her. Benny stuck his damp nose in her ear, and she laughed and draped an arm around his neck.

Jesse shook his head, planting his hands on his waist. "God. Well, I hope you *were* enjoying the peace and quiet." He glanced up at the sky, then down the beach. "I figured it would be safe to bring them along for my run, with the weather coming in. Usually they stick close, but I think Bosco recognized you."

"I'm flattered." She scratched his head as he vied with Benny for attention. "It's nice to have someone happy to see me."

"I'm happy to see you."

Butterflies bounced through her stomach, and she blinked at a sudden sting behind her eyes. *God. Get a grip.*

"Was the rest of your night okay?"

Heat spilled into her veins as she suddenly realized it had been less than 24 hours since he'd found her running around in the woods, confused and screaming. Lifting a shoulder, she pulled in a breath. "It was, actually. All was quiet. I slept on the couch, though." *In your shirt. Which I continued to wear all morning.* "I guess that's my new thing," she added quickly, hoping a little humor would distract him from the flush turning into fire beneath the skin of her cheeks.

He chuckled, but his expression turned serious. "Well, my offer stands. You know, if you ever want to crash in the guest bedroom."

She nodded, biting down on her lip. "Thanks." Pausing, she debated with herself before plunging ahead. "Actually, something weird did happen today, but it gave me an idea. An idea about how to stop all this, maybe. I wanted to run it by you, when you have time."

He tilted his head, raising his palms. "I've got time." He gestured toward the blanket, sitting down beside her when she moved over.

"Are you sure? I don't want to keep you from your run."

He raised a muscular shoulder in a shrug. "It can wait. The worst thing that will happen is two wet dogs." He tipped his head toward Bosco and Benny, who had wandered over to the high tide line to sniff at the tangles of seaweed and broken crab shells. "It's probably inevitable anyway," he added with a wry grin.

"You're sure?"

His brows pulled together. "Absolutely. Tell me what's going on, Lark."

She combed her fingers through her hair, trying to scrape loose strands back into the elastic tie as she gathered her thoughts. Why was she bringing him into this, after deciding this afternoon not to try to involve him anymore?

Her inner voice threw silent answers back at her in rapid-fire succession: because he was already involved, having come to her rescue last night. Because he'd grown up right next to the house. Because his mother was looking into the family history for her. Because he seemed to want to help. Because he was sitting right next to her, his bare arm nearly brushing hers, putting off his run to hear what she had to say.

Because she needed someone to talk to.

And because she wanted that someone to be him.

There it was—the painful truth. She wanted to be close to him, to share things with him, to strengthen this fragile connection growing between them. And that was dangerous. Her battered heart couldn't take anymore. Her trampled ego couldn't take anymore. It was too risky, and she was leaving soon anyway.

Still, he was waiting for her to speak, and the silence was verging on awkward. She twisted her fingers together, blowing out a breath. "So, remember I told you about a picture falling off the wall? It was a portrait of the pastor, John. And I think that has some significance."

"I remember. And that makes sense. But you said something else happened?"

"Yes. This morning, I was doing a little research, and something else fell off that wall. A wooden cross." She shuddered, looking out across the water. Whitecaps formed as the ocean chop intensified. "And it fell right after..." she trailed off, feeling silly. He's a vet, she reminded herself. "Well, I was talking out loud, to the cat...and I said something about maybe there really weren't any ghosts in the house."

"Whoa." He touched her back, his palm sliding across her shoulder blades. "That must have been pretty terrifying. Are you okay?"

"Yeah, it was, but I'm fine." Her skin heated beneath his touch, and she lost her train of thought for a moment. "Anyway, I came up with a theory. If there is really a ghost, and it's John, maybe he's trying to send me a message because he needs something. No one's been in that house long-term in a while. Maybe this is his chance."

"Sounds plausible." Jesse gave her shoulder a squeeze, then lowered his hand to the sand behind her, leaning back on his arms. The last of the beachgoers had disappeared, and the dogs were attempting to drag a large piece of driftwood out of the surf. "Hope they don't think they're bringing that home," he muttered under his breath. "So, what do you think he's trying to tell you?"

"Well, after the cross fell, I noticed an old picture of his church on the shelf. And all the gravestones around the building made me realize that he must be buried there too. I mean, he was the pastor there for years, right? But the thing is...he committed suicide. What if he wasn't given a proper Christian burial, since he took his own life?"

Jesse's forehead creased. "You mean, because it was considered a sin?"

"Exactly. So I did a little research this afternoon, and apparently the Church of England did have a law about suicide. Up until a few years ago, it was forbidden to give people who had killed themselves a standard Christian burial. The clergy were supposed to use an alternate service in those cases. I realize a few quick searches doesn't make me an expert, but John's church, that historic one up the hill from Main Street, is Congregational. And the Congregationalist Church was founded on the idea that each church makes its own decisions for that individual parish, often with input from the members. If I'm understanding everything correctly, that means whoever took over as the new pastor would have made the decision, maybe along with the rest of the parish, on what service Pastor John would receive at his burial."

"Which means it's possible he received the alternate service."

"Right. And you mentioned last night that some people believed he killed his wife. So between that and him definitely taking his own life, I wouldn't be surprised if that's what they decided. But if he was guilty of nothing more than being terribly depressed and unable to go on, maybe his spirit needs the real thing in order to rest."

"There must be records. We should go talk to the current pastor."

Gratitude bubbled through her at his use of "we". Why was a busy veterinarian willing to spend his time unraveling some ghost mystery that really had nothing to do with him? Despite what he'd said last night, she didn't really think he believed in haunted houses. Then again, she hadn't either, until very recently.

"And if it turns out he didn't get the standard Christian service, maybe..." She cut herself off, unable to bring herself to use the word "we". Casting about for a way to finish her sentence without making assumptions, she added, "Then maybe that could be arranged now."

"It's worth a shot." He sat forward, laying a hand on her wrist. "I was worried about you last night, Lark." He held her gaze, his dark blue eyes shining with intensity. The wind lifted his hair, revealing lines of concern across his forehead.

She swallowed. "I'm sorry."

"Don't be sorry," he said, his voice taking on a rough edge. "I just want to know you're safe."

Nodding, she chewed on her bottom lip. "I'll do some more

reading tonight, just to make sure I have as much information as possible before I start asking the church to redo 60-year-old burial services." She looked away, glancing at the approaching thunderheads. "I was in a hurry earlier...I wanted to get here before the storm hit."

"I like to watch the storms come in too." He gestured toward her camera case. "Were you going to take photos?"

An inexplicable bolt of panic shot through her, as though to admit she was taking photos again out loud would expose a piece of herself she wasn't entirely sure she was ready to resurrect. She inhaled slowly, glancing at the camera. Taking a few pictures didn't mean she was committed to anything. But then again, it felt like reclaiming something meaningful...something Nathan and Brittney *hadn't* taken from her.

"Yes," she finally said, reaching for the camera case like it was a life raft in a maelstrom of emotions. Once she had it in her hands, she felt more in control. Stronger. She took the camera out and checked the settings. "I already took a few." She glanced up at the dogs, who had abandoned the driftwood and wandered a little ways down the deserted beach. "I could take some of Bosco and Benny, if you'd like."

"I'd love that. I could hang them in the clinic."

She smiled as a rush of pleasure pulsed through her. Unfurling her legs, she pushed herself up to standing, adjusting the hem of her short dress. "I should get a little closer," she said, tipping her chin toward the dogs.

Jesse walked beside her down the beach, but when the dogs caught sight of them, they raced back, Bosco in the lead. The pit bull took a quick detour to chase a fleeing seagull, then continued to tear across the sand. As he reached them, he cut a sharp circle around their legs, knocking into the side of Lark's knee. She weaved sideways, latching on protectively to the camera strap hanging over her shoulder. A sudden jolt of pain flared as the ball of her foot landed on a jagged shell, and she stumbled, crying out.

Strong arms caught her before she fell. "Sit!" Jesse commanded, shooting a stern glance at the dogs. His voice and expression softened as he turned his attention back to her. "Are you okay?"

"Oh, yes, I'm fine." She looked up at him, her breath catching as she met his concerned gaze. "Just...lost my balance. Stepped on a shell." Her ability to make full sentences seemed to be failing her at the moment. She couldn't think clearly this close to him.

"You want me to look at it?"

She shook her head slowly, unable to speak. Her heart skittered erratically as his hand slid up to cup her face. His thumb grazed her cheek, trailing a slow arc of heat across her skin. He drew her closer, his gaze falling to her mouth as he lowered his head.

Anticipation hummed between them, stretching the moment out until his lips brushed against hers. A tiny moan escaped her throat, and he deepened the kiss as she pressed herself against the hard planes of his chest. *Oh, God.*

His hand moved to the back of her head, anchoring her as his mouth claimed hers, and her knees turned to liquid. She was going to melt into a puddle right here in the sand. Tangling her fingers in his hair, she lifted onto her toes, straining to get closer to him. Desire coursed through her, hot and demanding. *Jesse.*

She didn't register the rain at first, only vaguely noticing the sensation of the cool drops on her flushed skin. Nothing mattered but Jesse. The sky could crack open, unleashing a torrential downpour, and she would remain in this moment, kissing him.

But a persistent thought kept trying to push its way in. Her camera. The rain. A remote part of her brain sent up an alarm, reminding her that she needed to protect the precious gift from her parents.

She tensed as reality rushed back in. What was she doing? She didn't just need to protect her camera—she needed to protect her heart.

He felt the change in her body and relaxed his hold on her, easing back slightly. "Everything okay?" he asked softly, his blue eyes filled with concern as he lifted his head.

"The rain...my camera," she managed, still dazed.

Understanding flashed across his handsome features. "Oh!" He immediately turned back in the direction they'd come, holding out his hand as they started hurrying toward the abandoned towel. "Here, give it to me. I'll put it under my shirt."

The rain quickly strengthened, pelting them with sharp drops as thunder rumbled overhead. She tore the strap off her shoulder and handed him the camera, and he tucked it under his shirt and rounded his back forward like a football player shielding the ball. The dogs ran with them, slightly panicked by their sudden flight and the ominous noises emanating from the sky.

When they reached her things, Jesse relinquished the camera, holding the towel above her like a makeshift tent as she bundled her camera into the case, wrapped it in a plastic bag, and secured it in the duffle bag. She pulled out her raincoat before zipping it closed, finally letting out a breath of relief. Blinking the raindrops from her lashes, she flicked a glance between her raincoat and her soggy dress. "I'm not sure I should bother, at this point," she said with a shrug, looking back at him.

An answering grin tugged at the corners of his mouth, and he dragged a hand through his damp hair. "Hey, it's better than nothing. Ready?" He reached for her duffle bag, hiking a thumb in the direction of the trail leading back to the street.

His T-shirt was plastered to his torso, and the sight of his muscled shoulders beneath the clinging fabric brought the kiss back to the forefront of her mind. She caught her swollen lower lip with her teeth, a potent mixture of pleasure and fear roiling through her. Seriously, what had she been thinking?

You weren't thinking. At all.

Out loud, she replied, "Ready." Hurrying across the wet sand beside him, she noticed as he shortened his stride to match hers, and a pang of gratitude tightened her chest. Why did he have to be so kind in addition to being so hot?

One way or another, he'll break your heart.

She couldn't let it happen again, couldn't let this go any further. She was leaving as soon as possible, and his life was here, working at the clinic he'd promised his father he'd maintain. If he didn't lose interest in her before that, they'd have to say goodbye then. And if he was only looking for a physical relationship…well, she wasn't sure at this point she'd be able to keep her emotions in check if they went that route. He was just too…everything.

The trail was too narrow to climb side-by-side, but he reached a hand out behind him to help her navigate the steep terrain, proving the points she was making in her internal argument with herself.

Her breathing grew ragged as they neared the top, and the wind slapped damp strands of hair against her face. She wondered what she must look like, with her topknot falling apart and her face red from exertion. Thankfully, she hadn't worn much makeup to work, so at least there wouldn't be mascara trailing black rivers down her cheeks.

They paused at the top of the dunes, and he gestured toward a lone pair of flip-flops lying by the seagrass. "Are those yours?" As she nodded, he added, "Is your foot going to be okay?"

"Yes, I think it's fine," she said, ignoring the tug at her heart his question elicited. She stuffed her toes into the straps, testing the ball of her foot against the sole. In all honesty, between the kiss and the rain, she'd completely forgotten about the pain in her foot. The spot was slightly tender, but nothing that would impair her walking. "I'm good." She shot him a playful grin, unable to resist. "If I said I wasn't, would you carry me back?"

"Absolutely," he replied as they set off down the sandy gravel road. "I did pretty well with the camera, didn't I?"

She laughed, trying not to picture him tucking her under

his shirt and hugging her to his chest. Dear God, what was wrong with her? "I weigh a little bit more than the camera."

"I'll try not to take that as a lack of confidence in my strength."

She giggled again, wiping her face with her hands. "Never. But I do think your carrying me might slow us down."

Lightening flashed, brightening the dark sky for a split second. She jumped, letting out a little gasp. Together, they sped up, their feet slapping through puddles as they approached the fork in the road. Either they parted ways here, to head to their individual driveways, or trekked through the woods, following the path along the river to their adjoining backyards.

The dogs made the decision for them, plunging into the woods. Jesse glanced at her, his brows lifted. "I think it's okay if we hurry. The lightening's still far off."

She nodded, following him onto the trail as thunder cracked overhead. Beneath the canopy of trees, they were sheltered from the full strength of the rain, and they slowed their pace slightly. To their left, the river churned along its route, waterlogged branches swirling on the surface. Lark pulled the hair tie from the crown of her head and shook out the sodden strands, attempting to comb through the tangled mess with her fingers. "Sorry about your run. I'm assuming this isn't what you had in mind."

He chuckled, but then his gaze turned serious as he locked eyes with her. "All in all, this wasn't so bad."

She flushed, looking down at her feet. Sand and pine needles clung to her moist skin, and one of the scratches from the other night had opened up, sending a stinging pain through the torn flesh. Had her wild run through the woods only been last night? It felt like ages ago.

"I didn't get the pictures of the dogs," she said to steer the conversation away from allusions to their kiss.

He lifted a shoulder. "Rain check?" With a grimace, he shook his head as he glanced at the sky. "Sorry, that wasn't intentional. Another time?"

She giggled. "Sure."

"Hey, why don't you come over for dinner one night this week? I could cook out, and fill you in on whatever my mom finds out about the house. I'm having dinner with her tomorrow."

More evidence of his kindness. In fact, it was a double whammy—he'd already asked his mom for help with Lark's situation, and he was taking his mom out to eat. If he was trying to make her fall for him, he was doing a good job. And now he was offering to cook *her* a meal too.

She should find a way to decline, before she was in too deep. Then again, he knew she was leaving town eventually, and it didn't seem to concern him. Maybe she was reading too much into his invitation.

There was no way she could say no, though...not with what was going on with the house. She needed to know what his mother had found out. And with his work schedule, she couldn't exactly suggest a less intimate setting—like the coffee place—for the conversation.

"That would be great," she finally said, suddenly aware she'd taken a little too long to answer.

"I have a meeting on Monday night, for a town board I'm on. Tuesday?"

She mentally ran through her work schedule for the upcoming week. She worked nights Sunday, Thursday, and Friday. "That works. Thanks, Jesse. I can't wait to hear what your mom discovers."

"I didn't speak to her very long today, but she said she knew a little history and she'd ask some friends with knowledge of the family too."

"I'll call the church, see if I can get an appointment to talk to someone. I'm not sure I can explain my needing 60-year-old burial information because of a haunting over the phone."

The bridge separating their property came into view, and she glanced through the trees at the back of her house. The sheeting rain and rising mist made it look especially creepy, and a shudder traveled through her.

"If you want me to come with you, see if you can make an evening appointment."

"Thanks," she said as they slowed at the bridge. They were on his side of the river, and the dogs turned expectantly toward their home. Benny took a moment to shake, sending a spray of water from his chocolate coat.

"Guess I'd better get them dried off and fed," he said, tipping his chin toward his backyard. "Will you be okay?"

She glanced longingly at his house, picturing sitting with him in the same room as last night, warm and dry and with hot drinks in their hands. *Stop.* Arranging her features in a confident expression, she nodded. "Yes. I'm looking forward to a hot shower and hopefully a quiet night."

"Me too." His gaze lingered on her for a moment as the rain pattered against the leaves overhead. Then another flash of lightening illuminated the sky, breaking the spell. "Okay. Call me if you need anything, okay? I'm right here."

"I will. Have a good night," she added, accepting the duffle bag as he handed it to her. Then she forced her feet to turn toward her own property and carry her across the bridge. As she climbed the hill, she allowed herself one quick peek backwards. But the sheets of rain and dark woods obscured any view of him. With a heavy sigh, she put her head down and trudged the rest of the way up the hill.

9

She was relieved to find nothing amiss when she entered the house, and when Preston followed her down into the kitchen after her shower, a little bit more of the tension fraying her nerves slipped away. Maybe the ghost had exhausted itself for the time being. Manipulating things in this world had to take energy. It couldn't pull tricks all day every day, could it? If that were the case, no one would have ever come here for vacations over the years, and she knew some of her family members had. Even she had had some peaceful nights here, although it seemed like those were few and far between now.

She poured a glass of wine, then wandered over to the sliding glass door, where Preston was perched on his cat tree. The bird feeder swayed in the wind, deserted by wildlife during the storm. The yard beyond the deck was shrouded in a veil of mist, the woods disappearing in the waning light.

Sipping her wine, she scratched Preston between the ears as she watched the night fall.

A bolt of lightning charged the air, illuminating the backyard like the flash of a camera. The effect made her suddenly remember the few photos she'd managed to take before the storm hit. *Before you started kissing Jesse*, a sly voice whispered in her head. She blew out a breath and made her way to the front of the house, where her duffle bag sat by the door. She'd removed the wet towel to stuff it in the washer, leaving her camera on the coffee table.

The mixture of the wine and the anticipation of looking at her pictures had her feeling slightly giddy as she sank onto the couch. Swallowing another healthy sip of the crisp Sauvignon Blanc, she traded the glass for the camera and leaned back into the cushions. She put her feet on the coffee table as she pulled up today's photos on the camera screen.

The most recent image came up, and she flipped through them in reverse order. There were a few decent ones, especially the shots from the vantage point of the top of the dunes. She studied one for a moment, chewing on her lip. That one was probably the best of them. Nodding to herself, she clicked through to the photos she'd snapped before she'd headed to the beach.

Her backyard filled the small screen, and she froze as her gaze snapped to the edge of the woods. What the hell? She blinked, pulling the camera closer to her face. A shadowy figure stood just inside the tree line, staring back at her. She sucked in a breath, nearly dropping the camera.

No one had been there, she was sure of it. It was just a trick of the light. Some strange combination of mist and overcast skies. With trembling fingers, she zoomed in on the hazy form. Her stomach lurched.

There was definitely something there, but...not quite *all* there. A human shape, pale and slightly out-of-focus, lurked near the entrance to the path. But the body wasn't solid—the vague shape of low branches shone through it, like fingers behind gauze. And it was almost completely monotone, made up of smoky shades of white and gray, with dark smudges for features and long, ashen hair.

She straightened her spine so suddenly an ominous crack broke the silence, an accompanying flare of pain lancing through her upper back. *It was a woman.* The figure in the woods was a ghost, and it was a woman.

The revelation pushed both disappointment and excitement to the forefront of her wildly swirling emotions, nearly overtaking fear. How could this be? She'd thought she had it figured out...thought there might be a solution. But if she'd captured the ghost's image—and it certainly appeared that way —she was dealing with a female spirit. Not Pastor John.

The hopelessness of the situation punched her in the gut. She was back to square one. Unless...maybe the ghost was Martha. But what did she want? Lark squinted at the camera screen again, checking the other shots of the backyard. The filmy figure appeared in each one that contained the woods. There was no doubt it was a woman...aside from the long hair, Lark could make out the blurred edges of a white dress.

She moaned, setting the camera on a cushion and clutching her stomach as she hunched forward. This was too much. She squeezed her eyes shut, rocking forward and back on the edge of the couch.

Something creaked overhead, and she whipped her head back to look up. "Please, no," she whispered, still hugging herself as she scanned the ceiling. "I can't handle anymore." A shudder crept up her spine as she realized what room was directly above her. The guest bedroom with the window overlooking the driveway. The one she'd had to check on her first day.

A soft tune seeped through the upstairs floorboards, and her blood turned to ice. Someone—*something*—was singing, the words low and muffled, intoned by the high pitch of a female voice. The lilting melody rose and fell in a repetitive rhythm that felt familiar. Recognition twisted through her in a sickening rush. A lullaby. *Oh, God.*

She dragged her gaze toward the staircase, rising slowly, as though some invisible force was now in control of her movements. Fear coursed through her veins, but still she drifted toward the stairs, compelled to follow the tune, to search out the disembodied voice. What choice did she have?

Run! A panicked inner voice responded. But where would she go? There was nowhere she could run to. This was her home now, and she had to deal with this herself. And Preston was here. She wouldn't abandon him.

She felt like a ghost herself as she climbed the stairs... insubstantial, untethered, alone. Despite her terror, she ascended each step as though under a spell. Turning left at the landing, she continued down the hallway, pulled by an unrelenting tide.

The door to the front bedroom loomed ahead, closed, just as she always left it. As she approached, the singing grew slightly louder, although the words remained indistinct. The tune was unmistakable, however—Rock-a-bye Baby.

She gripped the knob, every inch of her flesh covered in goosebumps. *If something happens to me, Jesse will make sure Preston's okay.* He was a vet. He would find him a good home. Or maybe adopt Preston himself.

The eerie melody was going to drive her mad. Before she could change her mind, she shoved the door open. A wall of cold crashed into her, and she gasped, slapping at the light switch.

A figure sat on the far bed, facing away, toward the rain-spattered window. Long hair woven into a braid fell down the back of a white dress.

The scream lodged in Lark's throat tore from her lips, and she reeled backwards. As her cry split the air, the specter vanished, the hushed lyrics of the lullaby fading with it.

She caught her balance and stared into the room, blinking. Despite seeing the woman in the photograph, some part of her brain still scrambled to blame her imagination. Had she really just seen a ghost? Her gaze lingered on the now-empty bed, then dropped to the comforter. The material along the edge of the bed now bunched into a faint depression, as if to prove someone had been sitting there moments before.

Nausea swirled through her like acid as she backed away, pulling the door closed. That was it. There would be no sleeping for her tonight. She could sleep tomorrow...maybe on the beach.

With a shuddering sigh, she backed down the hallway, keeping the closed door in view until the last possible minute. Then she hurried into the bathroom and scooped up a few things, taking a quick moment to check that Preston's bowls were filled. She'd make sure the ones in the kitchen were full as well, just in case he had reservations about coming up here tonight. She knew she wasn't returning to the top floor. An entire opera could play out and she still wasn't going to venture back upstairs until the sun was out.

Shut up, she hissed at the inner voice reminding her that strange things had happened during the daylight hours as well. Right now she just had to focus on making it through the night. Another voice played out in her head—the reassuring memory of her father's unwavering confidence in her abilities. He'd been fierce in his belief that she learn to rely on herself, but always kind and supportive with his message. Okay. She was a grown-up. Anyone would be frightened in this situation —any sane person, that was—but she could handle fear.

A pang of grief tightened her chest as she remembered, once again, that the only way she'd ever hear his words from now on was in her own mind. She stopped short by the couch, wrinkling her brow. If this ghost could appear to her, why couldn't her father? Or her mother, for that matter?

This ghost needs something from you. She chewed her lip, glancing up toward the ceiling, and a slender thread of sympathy twisted itself into the knot of tangled emotions. What if one of her parents needed something from a living person? Lark would want that person to help, if they could.

She scrubbed her face. If this ghost was Martha, that was

her great aunt. A relative, however distant. Exhaling, she sank onto the couch, picking up her abandoned wine. At least thinking about this whole thing in more practical terms made her feel slightly better.

The urge to call Jesse was nearly overwhelming, and she fought to shut the thought down as she dragged her gaze away from her cell phone. He was not her protector, no matter how kind he was. Being around him was risky, especially after what had happened only hours earlier. So far, she'd been okay in this house, despite the haunting. She would probably survive a ghost.

She would not survive another heartbreak.

She curled her knees into her chest as she leaned into the cushions, gazing out the window. Rain continued to slide down the panes, but the thunder and lightning had passed. Hopefully the sun would return in the morning, and a peaceful nap on the beach would be possible. Because at the moment, she couldn't imagine her heartrate slowing to a rhythm compatible with sleep, and she certainly didn't think she would be able to avoid seeing the image of the phantom woman if her eyes closed.

It was going to be another long, sleepless night. With a sigh of acceptance, she reached for the television remote.

$\mathcal{B}$oth dogs lifted their heads in unison, noses turning toward the woods. Jesse glanced up from the grill and caught a flash of movement between the trees. A moment later, Lark appeared on the path, and the dogs took off across the lawn to greet her. She returned his wave and bent to pet the dogs, their happy barks mixing with her laughter as they climbed the hill.

"Hey," she called as she approached, a smile lighting up her face. The sleeveless copper blouse she wore highlighted the dark fire of her hair and the soft glow of her creamy skin. Tiny black shorts revealed her shapely legs, and a delicate gold chain adorned one ankle.

His body stirred as he stared at her, and he had to resist the urge to pull her into an embrace. They weren't there yet, despite Saturday's kiss. If anything, she'd seemed desperate to create distance between them—both physically and emotionally—after it had happened. But during...well, he definitely *hadn't* imagined the heat and chemistry between them. She'd kissed him back with a fierceness that surprised him, her desire matching his, sexy sounds escaping her throat as she clung to him.

He pushed the memory away before the warmth surging through his blood had a chance to betray his thoughts. "Hi. I hope the welcoming crew behaved appropriately."

She giggled, scratching the top of Benny's brown head. "There were a few rogue sniffs, but overall, I'll give them a ten out of ten for enthusiasm."

Laughing with her, he flipped the burgers on the grill. The flames flared, mixing with the heavy evening air, and he drew an arm across his forehead. "There's no question they're glad you're here." He glanced back up. "We all are."

She flushed, the pink stain darkening the faint freckles along her cheekbones. "Thanks for the invite. Can I do anything to help?" Unhooking a bag from her shoulder, she set it on the stone pavers of the patio.

"Nope. These shouldn't take too long, and the salad's already put together. Can I get you something to drink? Beer or wine?" He gestured with his own half-empty bottle of beer. "A local brew, if you want to try it. IPA."

"Sure, I'll try it. But let me get it while you're doing that."

"Right here in the cooler," he said, setting down the long spatula and walking over to the back door. Opening the cooler, he dug a bottle from the bed of ice and twisted it open for her. "Cheers," he added, handing it to her.

She raised the bottle in answer to his toast before taking a sip, then nodded. "It's really good. And the burgers smell amazing."

"Thanks. I'm not much of a cook, but I can manage this much."

"Oh! I baked something." Reaching into her tote bag, she pulled out a plastic-wrapped loaf. "I hope you like banana bread."

"Wow, thank you." Their hands touched as he accepted the bread, and their eyes locked. She bit her lower lip, lifting one shoulder in a small half-shrug, and his gaze slid down to her mouth. He wanted to kiss those lips, badly. *Control yourself.* A loaf of banana bread was not an invitation to ravish her.

She swallowed. "It's the least I could do."

"It wasn't necessary, but I'm glad you did. I love banana bread. My mom used to make it."

"Mine too," she said, her voice catching. A shadow of grief flashed across her face before it was replaced with a small smile. "Did you have a nice dinner with your mom the other night?"

His chest tightened as he remembered she had no family left. Once again, he wanted to wrap his arms around her, this time as a comfort. All his training, both military and medical, had molded him into the role of protector, and feeling powerless to help was difficult. But she had already moved the conversation on, and he sensed any sympathy might make her feel too vulnerable.

"I did, thanks. And she did tell me a few things she learned about your relatives." At least that information, however sparse, might help Lark in some small way.

Hope lit up her green eyes. "Really?"

Nodding, he held up a package of cheese slices as he lifted his brows in a silent question.

"Yes, please. And I'm anxious to hear what you found out."

"I don't know how helpful it's going to be, but I can fill you in while we eat, unless you'd rather wait until after dinner."

"No need to wait. I live with a ghost, so not much fazes me these days." The corner of her mouth scrunched into a weary sideways grin as she lifted the beer bottle to her lips.

That sense of humor. Even if they were only destined to be friends, he would miss her if she moved.

When she moved, a firm inner voice reminded him as he slid the burgers onto a platter. They fixed their plates and sat at the patio table, the dogs positioning themselves beside their chairs in the hopes of catching any dropped pieces of food.

After he made sure she had everything she needed and asked about how Preston was doing, he pulled his cell from the back pocket of his shorts and set it on the table. "Sorry," he said, tilting his chin toward the phone as he tapped on the notes app. "I just want to make sure I don't forget anything."

"No worries. I'm glad you wrote it down." She lifted her cheeseburger to her lips, adding, "These are really good." Beside her, Benny shifted his weight to sit up taller, his soulful eyes trained on her movements.

"Thanks." He had to admit, they were pretty good. With an exasperated sigh, he nodded toward Benny. "Let me know if he's being too annoying."

She shook her head as she finished chewing. "He's fine," she said with a little laugh.

He hated to bring down the light mood, but he knew she wanted to hear the details he'd received from his mother, so he scanned his notes to remind himself what she'd said. "Okay, so my mother spoke with a few of her friends at the retirement community, primarily two women who lived in Truro most of their lives. But between the three of them, they have some ideas on who else to talk too." He glanced up at her with an apologetic smile. "I hate to say it, since their mystery is your reality, but this is the most exciting thing that's happened over there for a while."

She bobbed her head in a small nod. "I get it. It *is* pretty fascinating, if you take out the having to live there part."

He was tempted to reiterate his invitation to crash in the guest room, but he didn't want to push her. He'd already told her—more than once—she was welcome to stay with him; hopefully she would keep the offer in mind. "Exactly. And I will say I didn't give my mom a full account of everything that's happened, since it's not really my place to tell her all the details."

"I appreciate that," she said, her voice tinged with gratitude and relief.

An ache opened in his chest at her reaction to this minor act of respect. "Of course. My mom may not live in Truro anymore, but the Cape Cod community is still pretty small." He took a swig of his beer. "Not that anything that's happening with that house reflects badly on you...it's just up to you who you choose to discuss it with."

She blinked rapidly, the slim column of her throat moving

as she swallowed hard. Swiping at the corner of her eye, she reached for her beer as well.

Was she holding back tears? He wanted to reach out and squeeze her hand, but she was sitting across from him, the table keeping them at a distance. *Damn it.* Frustration coiled through him, his fingers tightening around the cool glass of the bottle instead of her warm flesh. The only thing he could think of to ease her emotional response was to draw attention away from it, so he plunged into the story his mom had relayed.

"Anyway, the house was built around 1946, after the war had ended. The Holloways had been living in a small house owned by the parish, but apparently Martha's health was pretty delicate, so they felt getting her out of such an old building with a few centuries of dust and mold would be a good idea. Oh, and they were hoping to start a family, so a bigger place would be necessary for that as well. One of my mom's friends said that according to the grapevine, Martha had already had multiple miscarriages."

"Oh!"

He glanced up, his brows raising to match hers. "What?"

She grimaced, her expression turning apologetic. "Yikes. I mean…that's so sad. Sorry. It's just that…well, the miscarriages might explain something. I still need to fill you in on that. But I'd like to hear what else your mom found out," she added, leaning forward.

He nodded, clamping down the rising concern as he checked his notes. *What else had happened over there since Saturday?* Clearing his throat, he continued. "I guess at that point, Martha was doing poorly enough to warrant help, so the bigger house also meant they were able to have someone move in to help her with housework, cooking, shopping, that kind of stuff. No one seemed to know exactly what was wrong with Martha—she was somewhat private—but the guess is maybe some kind of autoimmune issue, possibly combined with depression or something else related to her mental health."

A mosquito whined in his ear, and he swiped at it. "Let's see...what else? You've probably found the obits online already, but my mom looked them up too. Martha died on September 6th, 1950. Keep in mind, my mom hadn't even been born at this point, but some of the older ladies at the retirement community were children then, and of course there was always gossip about the house. So the general story is that Martha woke up in the middle of the night, got out of bed, and fell on her way downstairs."

He paused as an uninvited image slid into his mind: a crumpled body, head twisted at an impossible angle, lying right beyond the open door where he and Lark had said goodbye on Friday night. Their gazes locked, and he could tell from Lark's expression she was picturing the same thing. A sinking feeling pulled at his stomach, but there was nothing to be done. Talking about ghosts meant talking about dead people—there was no way around it. Still, he hurried to move the conversation away from Martha and her broken neck.

"Um...after the accident, John stayed on as pastor for another five years, until his decline reached a point where the parish decided he had to be replaced. He...well, you know. He hung himself in 1960." *Crap.* That imagery wasn't any better.

And he was about to make it worse. He hesitated, debating whether to reveal the rest of the details.

"It's okay. I can take it," she said after a few beats of silence.

What choice did he have? This was her house, her mystery. Her relative. Blowing out a breath, he continued. "Right. Sorry, it's just that it's a bit grisly. Okay, so like I was saying, he hung himself in 1960 inside the house, off the hallway bannister. At that point, he had become very reclusive, and he lived alone, so no one found him for a while."

Some of the color leached from her face as she nodded, lips pressed together. Reaching for her beer, she took a healthy swallow.

He slapped at a mosquito hovering near his calf. The light was fading as dusk settled in, bringing with it the irritating insects. He'd have to get them inside soon. "Anyway, he *was* buried in the church cemetery, but my mom and her friends don't know anything about what kind of service it was. One thing did occur to me, though...Mom mentioned that the consensus seems to be that rumors about ghosts began shortly after Martha died. John would have still been alive, which means if there was a haunting going on then, it wasn't him. I don't know if that means it's not him *now*, but it's something to think about." He shrugged, sliding his phone back into his pocket.

"It's not him," she said, shaking her head. "My theory was wrong."

He blinked, momentarily taken aback by this turn of events. So something significant *had* happened since Saturday. Why hadn't she come to him immediately? The concern he'd pushed aside returned, mixed with something less noble—disappointment that she hadn't wanted to share whatever she'd discovered right away. They'd exchanged texts for the past few days, mostly about dinner plans, but there had been no mention of any revelations. She'd simply assured him she was okay whenever he asked.

He forced his taut muscles to relax. She *was* okay. She was sitting right here across from him. Just because he'd offered to help didn't mean she owed him anything. And it had already become fairly clear she was reluctant to depend on anyone. She might be mostly alone in the world, but she was also strong and independent.

He respected that. Respected her. But at the same time, he wanted her to trust him. And there was no denying he cared about her—he simply couldn't stop himself from worrying about her, alone in that haunted house.

Trust takes time, he reminded himself. And she was leaving.

She was here right now, though, and she was ready to tell him. That had to count for something.

He recovered himself before the delay in his response became awkward. "It was? You mentioned you needed to fill me in on something."

"I do. The good news though, if you want to call it that, is that I think I have a new theory now. What you just told me seems to support it." A mosquito landed on the bare skin of her shoulder, and she brushed it away absent-mindedly.

"Good. We should probably head inside, though, if you're finished?" He gestured at their plates.

She nodded, and they began gathering everything off the

table, the dogs at their heels as they made trips inside. Once all the food was in, she grabbed her tote bag, and he snagged two more beers from the cooler before closing the screen door against the bugs. He offered her one, handing it to her as she set her bag on the kitchen island.

"So...what happened?" He stood across from her, leaning back against the counter.

She fished through her bag for a moment before pulling out a small rectangle. "Remember Saturday?"

"I do," he replied, unable to keep a roguish grin from tugging at his lips.

A flush rose on her cheeks as she returned his smile. "Right. Well, I took some photos of the house, and the property, before I went down to the beach. I need to show you something." She held up the object, revealing a flash drive. "Do you have a computer we can use?"

His pulse accelerated as trepidation sliced through him. Show him something? He didn't like the sound of that. Pushing himself away from the counter, he tipped his head toward the laptop charging in the corner of the room. "Laptop okay? Or I have a bigger computer in my office."

She followed his gaze. "That should be fine."

He carried it over and set it in front of her on the island, quickly typing in the security code before stepping aside to let her insert the flash drive.

"So, after I got home on Saturday night, I pulled out my camera to look at my photos. And when I got to the ones of the woods in my backyard...well, let's just say it was a bit of a shock." Opening the folder, she scrolled through the thumbnail images before clicking on one. Her backyard filled the screen, and she turned it toward him.

He leaned forward, his gaze scanning the image. Whoa. What the hell? Squinting, he bent his head closer to the screen. A figure lurked along the edge of the woods, staring out from the tree line. But it wasn't...solid. It looked more like the *suggestion* of a person—translucent and hazy, with blurred features and an eerie luminosity. Still, it was distinct enough to rule out a trick of light, and to pick out a few details. Like a white dress. And long hair.

His stomach tightened. A ghost. A female ghost. The ramifications slammed into place. "It's not John because it's a woman," he said slowly.

"That's what it looks like to me. And she's in every one of the pictures of the back woods."

"I can't believe you caught a ghost on film." The hairs on the back of his neck prickled, and he reached back to rub the sensation away.

"I can't either. Well, I mean, figure of speech aside, I *can* believe it, because of everything that's been happening to me. But anyone else will just assume I photoshopped it." She caught his gaze, her emerald eyes seeking reassurance in his. "I swear I didn't do that."

"I would never think that, Lark." And truly, he didn't. It was surprising how easily he was accepting that some kind of supernatural phenomenon was going on over there. Despite being a man of science, he didn't find it impossible to believe there were forces in this world beyond his understanding. Especially after everything he'd heard about the house on the other side of the river, both over the years and in the past few days. Not to mention what he'd seen with his own eyes—her struggle in the woods, and now this. Actual photos.

She shrugged. "I wouldn't blame you if you did. I mean… you don't know me very well. This could just be my warped way of attention-seeking."

He touched her arm. "I definitely don't think that's what you're doing."

Their eyes remained locked as warmth flowed between their skin. She pulled in a shaky breath. "That's good, because I have something else to tell you."

Oh, no. The stormy look on her face told him it wasn't something good. "I'm listening," he said, giving her a reassuring squeeze before he let his hand fall away.

She swallowed audibly. "Right as I discovered the photos, I heard…singing." A shudder traveled through her.

"Singing?" Dread pooled in his belly.

"Yes. Coming from upstairs. A lullaby—Rock-a-bye Baby."

"Oh, Lark," he murmured, unable to think of anything else to say.

"It was a woman's voice, coming from that front bedroom where I saw the face the day I moved in. So I went up to check."

His muscles tightened as he pictured her alone in that house, climbing the stairs to investigate a ghostly voice as the storm lashed outside. *Why hadn't she called him?*

"When I opened the door, the room was freezing. The singing stopped, but right before it did, I saw…" Her voice broke, and she twisted her hands together, gathering herself before she continued. "I saw a woman, sitting on the bed. She had her back to me, but I saw the long hair. And the white dress. Then she vanished, but I could still see an imprint on the comforter, as if a real person had been sitting there and left a depression." She closed her eyes for a long moment.

He could no longer resist. "Why didn't you call me?" he asked gently, reaching for her hand.

"I wanted to." The words tumbled out quickly, and she bit down on her lip, as though she could catch them and reel them back.

"Then why didn't you?"

She shook her head even as she gripped his hand. "I don't want to be a burden. It's not how I was raised. My father always taught me to be self-reliant."

Understanding dawned. He bent forward until she meet his gaze. "It's a good lesson," he agreed softly. "But this isn't like being able to support yourself or knowing how to work a fire extinguisher. There's something very scary happening, and I happen to know you don't know anyone else in town." His tone took on a firmer note. "I *want* to be here for you. Do you believe me?"

"I…" She blinked rapidly, taking a breath. "Let's just say I've been disappointed before."

There it was. Someone had hurt her, badly. Anger for the unknown person bubbled up like acid, but he pushed it down. Right now, it was about making sure Lark understood that *he* wouldn't disappoint her. And that he had no ulterior motives.

"Lark, I care about you. I don't think it's any secret I'm attracted to you, but even if we're just friends, I still want to help. And maybe you don't know me all that well either, but I don't say things I don't mean."

Emotions played across her face. Her lips parted, but she only nodded, the silence stretching out as their fingers twined together.

A tremor crept into her voice as she spoke. "I'm attracted to you, too. I'm just…scared. Of getting too close."

She lived in a haunted house, and this was what she was scared of. His heart contracted. "Do you want to talk about it?"

Shaking her head, she moved closer. "No. I definitely don't want to talk about it." Her eyes darkened as she looked up at him. "Actually, I don't want to talk about anything at all."

His body stirred, responding to the current sparking between them. But he forced himself to make sure he was reading her signals correctly. "Are you sure?" he asked, reaching up with his free hand to tuck a lock of hair behind her ear.

A sound of assent, low and seductive, came from deep in her throat, and his blood heated. She lifted her mouth toward his, and he plunged his fingers into her thick auburn waves, cradling the back of her head as their lips crashed together. Need pounded through his veins, and he pulled her closer, desperate to feel every inch of her body against his.

They kissed each other hungrily, with the fierce urgency of a forbidden act. Her nails dug into his shoulders, driving him crazy. He wanted to feel her fingertips against his bare flesh, wanted to feel her warm skin sliding against his. Her soft moans were driving him wild, and he pressed her back against the edge of the island. He needed to get her into bed. Now.

She ground her hips against his, igniting a surge of exquisite agony. *Holy hell*. He slid his hand down her lower back and over the curve of her bottom, catching the back of her thigh as her bent knee hiked up toward his waist. The warmth of her soft, taut flesh filling his palm triggered a groan deep in his chest.

A mechanical trill cut through the rush of blood in his ears, and a dim part of his brain registered his cellphone ring. *No.* He ignored it even as he felt her tense in his arms. The sound continued, and despite his best efforts, the implications of not answering it began to pierce the heavy fog of desire. For anyone else, it might not be a problem. But he was the town's only vet, it was after hours, and his cell phone number was listed as the number to call in an emergency.

He tore his lips from hers, muttered curses mingling with apologies as he touched his forehead to hers.

"I understand," she murmured, pulling away slightly as he snatched the offending device off the island. An unknown number; not local. He swiped the screen, gripping the phone with a bit too much force as he lifted it to his ear. "Holt," he said roughly.

"Is this the vet?" The woman's voice was filled with barely contained hysteria.

Oh, crap. He stared down into Lark's eyes, hoping his expression conveyed what was going on as he said, "Yes, this is Dr. Holt," into the phone.

"I think my dog's been poisoned," the woman cried. "We're at a rental house, and I don't know what he could have gotten into. But he's vomiting and convulsing and I don't know what to do!" The last sentence rose to a wail that Lark could hear, and she frowned up at him, her flushed features clouded with concern.

Something inside him shifted, and it took him a moment to process it as he gave instructions to the desperate woman on the phone. Despite the interruption, despite the bad timing that would now end their night, Lark wasn't mad. There wasn't the slightest hint of annoyance on her face or in her demeanor; only a genuine look of distress that made his chest tighten. And he didn't think for one minute she didn't feel the same ache of frustration he was currently experiencing…it was just that she understood his obligations, understood that someone else's pet emergency would have to take precedence. After all, she'd been in a similar position when she'd first called him. But not everyone would immediately react in such a sincerely self-less way. With that realization, he understood that his feelings for her had moved beyond simply just caring about her.

He ended the call, acutely aware that his own body still wasn't ready to accept this turn of events. Grimacing, he tugged at his shorts, trying to will the painful throbbing away. He'd need to change into long pants to ride his bike; that would give him a minute. But he had to get moving. "I have to—"

"I know. I understand, I really do. I hope you can save the dog."

He reached out and touched her hand. "Sorry."

"It's fine. Really."

He hesitated, torn. The gentleman in him wanted to offer her a ride; make sure she made it home safe. The doctor in him was firmly reiterating that the clock was ticking, and bringing her home on the bike would take him in the opposite direction of the clinic for a few minutes. That could be life or death for the dog. *Damn it*. This wasn't a situation he'd dealt with before.

She read his mind. "Go," she instructed, squeezing his hand before releasing it and gesturing toward the front of the house. "I'm fine. I'll finish cleaning up. You need to hurry."

He did. He turned and strode toward the stairs, calling over his shoulder. "Don't worry about clean up, Lark. Leave now, okay? I just want to make sure you get home safe." He reminded himself that she'd arrived on her own perfectly fine. It was just that now it was dark. And he'd seen an actual photograph of something lurking in the woods. Then again, that thing in the woods lived in her house. *Damn it to hell.* "Will you text me as soon as you're home?"

"I'll be fine," she called back. "I'll leave now. Just hurry. And yes, I'll text."

*S*he tucked the house key into a little pocket in her leggings, zipping it closed as she strode down the driveway. Seemed a little silly to lock the door when the biggest threat to her safety appeared to be inside, but habits from the city died hard. Breaking into a jog, she did her best to focus on the rough terrain of the driveway to avoid injury. The last thing she needed was to step into a ditch and break an ankle, or trip on a root and go flying. She'd been distracted her entire shift today, and she knew exactly why.

She'd hoped by this evening she would have stopped thinking about Jesse. Or at least stopped thinking about him every ten minutes. No such luck. That kiss... *God.* That kiss was so hot, she couldn't even imagine what sleeping with him would be like. Although her mind certainly was trying.

Lifting her hand, she brushed her fingertips across her lips, still tender from last night's devouring kiss. A flush that had nothing to do with exercise warmed her cheeks. She snatched her hand away and leapt over a wide rut in the sandy dirt. Honestly, she had no one to blame but herself. She'd instigated things this time. Part of her was angry with herself, but it was a small part. There was no denying this kind of attraction. She simply didn't have even a tenth of the willpower it would take to stop herself if they ended up in that situation again. Truthfully, she didn't even want to stop herself. Every part of her body was aching for him. She would just need to keep her distance emotionally. That way, when it was time to say goodbye...whether because she was leaving, or whether because things had just run their course, it wouldn't hurt.

She could manage that. She was strong. Nathan and Brittney had taught her how strong she really was. They'd hurt her —nearly broken her—but she'd survived. And learned a valuable lesson.

A disgusted sigh escaped as she thought of those two. They deserved each other. And Nathan...he'd never kissed her the way Jesse had, not even in the beginning. Like he'd just crossed a desert and she was water. Heat surged through her lower body and she sped up, as if she could outpace her desire for Jesse. Good luck.

Seriously, what had she even been thinking, saying yes to Nathan's proposal? Why had he even asked? She'd been vulnerable after her parents' death, and he'd been...what? Taking the next logical step? Complying with his family's expectations? Keeping up with his newly married friends? Who knew, exactly? The whole thing had been a mess, they'd just been too close to see it.

If only Brittney hadn't been involved. To lose her best

friend as well as her fiancé in one fell swoop had been a huge blow. The two of them, betraying her like that, had shattered her trust in people. She was forever damaged. But that didn't mean she couldn't seek pleasure when she wanted it, as long as she remembered to keep the walls around her battered heart strong and tall. She pictured a mediaeval fortress inside her chest and smiled grimly. Maybe she could even add a moat.

She wished she had her parents to talk to about all this. Or anyone, for that matter. Maybe she'd call Madison later. She probably wouldn't discuss Jesse—and certainly not the paranormal stuff—but it would be good to chat with someone from home. She needed to nurture the friendships she had in the city for when she returned.

At least the ghost had left her alone last night. It had been quiet and she'd slept great, although Jesse had featured in several steamy dreams. They'd been texting frequently since last night, when she'd let him know she was home safe, as promised. He'd checked in later and let her know the dog was stable. A warm mix of relief and joy had spread through her at the news. Another emotion had snuck in, too...admiration. She was impressed with his abilities.

Then he'd called her this morning, when he'd had a lull at work, and they'd batted around some ideas about Martha. Maybe it hadn't been an accident or a murder...maybe she'd taken her own life after the emotional pain of the miscarriage. Maybe it was Martha who needed absolution in order to move on.

Either way, Lark was glad things had been quiet. This morning before her shift, she'd managed to set up a few appointments to get estimates on some of the work needed around the house. There was money in the trust designated for upkeep, but she had to be careful. She'd need to have enough for taxes, especially if it took a while to sell the house once she'd put it on the market.

Up ahead, a rabbit darted across the road, and she smiled to herself. She had to admit, it was nice seeing wildlife other than pigeons and squirrels, and the occasional rat. A flock of turkeys had been visiting her birdfeeder, drawn to the spilled seed. She'd been meaning to photograph them, but she was slightly concerned about what other images she might capture if she started taking more pictures of her backyard.

Her breathing became ragged as she pushed herself up the steep hill at the end of the road. From there, she'd head down the dunes and run along the beach. She'd thought about asking Jesse if he wanted to go with her, but he'd mentioned something about having practice tonight with his summer soccer league team.

As she made her way down toward the water, she did her best to clear her mind and appreciate the beauty surrounding her. The warm evening sun on her shoulders and the fresh, salty air in her lungs. Now that summer was in full swing, there were more people on the beach, even at this late hour.

Farther down the beach, a few people stood in a cluster, pointing out at the ocean, and she slowed to see what they were looking at. Seals were bobbing near the surf, their smooth dark heads popping up from the water as they searched for fish.

By the time she made her way back to the house, the sun

had disappeared behind the tree line, draining the sky of its golden hue and replacing it with shades of rose and violet. Soon it would be the 'blue hour', that time of day between sunset and twilight that photographers coveted. She briefly considered grabbing her camera and setting up some shots, but she was tired and dripping with sweat. Instead, she let herself into the house and wandered into the kitchen. Grabbling a bottle of water, she sank into a chair at the little table. As she guzzled the water, she reached for a few sheets of paper from the top of a pile and fanned her face. Perspiration ran in rivulets from her temples and the back of her neck. As soon as she had cooled down, she'd jump in the shower.

Her gaze landed on a corner of paper she'd revealed when she'd disturbed the pile. The family tree she'd created. The euphoria derived from exercise seeped away by a few degrees as her thoughts turned back to her parents. Once again, she wished it was one of them trying to connect with her from beyond, and not a distant relative she'd never known. Still, it helped to keep in mind that Martha was a relative, and hopefully didn't mean Lark any harm. She just needed to find out what it was she wanted. Or needed.

"What is it you need, Martha?" she murmured, her heart rate speeding back up as she realized she'd spoken aloud. That had gotten her into trouble before. Then again, communication might be the only way to solve this. It was just probably a bad idea to invite that communication after the sun had gone down.

Sighing, she pushed herself up, passing Preston's cat tower and giving him a quick pat before she climbed the stairs. She allowed herself a long shower, luxuriating in the warm spray of water over her sore muscles. It probably would have been an even better idea to take a bath, she realized as she rinsed conditioner from her hair. A long soak in the tub sounded decadent. Maybe tomorrow night after work.

As she stepped out of the shower, the bathroom lights flickered, and she froze, her breath catching. Uh oh. She remained motionless, as if that might keep anything else from happening, her towel clutched against her damp chest. Another quick sputter plunged her into total darkness, and she blinked against the sudden curtain of black.

Before she could react, the lights returned—slowly, as if someone was increasing the power strength by reversing a dimmer switch. The breath she'd been holding came out in a painful whoosh. Maybe just a power surge? It was an old house.

You spoke to Martha, a chastising inner voice reminded her. You literally asked her what she needed. Idiot. She opened the towel and wrapped it around herself, securing it in a knot. Okay. Everything was fine. Still, she'd prefer to hurry up and get out of this room. Stepping in front of the sink, she swiped at the steam fogging the surface of the mirror.

The face that stared back at her was not her own.

The eyes were brown, not green. No dusting of freckles across the cheekbones. Pointier chin, thinner lips, higher forehead. Long hair that was brown, not red. *And not wet.*

Lark screamed, and suddenly it was her own face in the mirror—her familiar features, her green eyes, wide with fear but recognizable. No sign of the intruder. Still, she spun around, her heart flailing like a trapped bird.

No one was there. Reaching back, she gripped the sink with trembling hands. What was happening? Or rather, *who* was happening? The rogue face was already fading from her memory, but she was certain of one thing: the mysterious woman in the mirror had been young. Younger than Lark. If it was Martha, it was a young Martha. Was that how ghosts worked?

Before she could change her mind, before she lost the details, she raced through the hall and into her bedroom. Slowing at the door to the study, she scanned the room, then cautiously approached the portrait of Martha. It still hung on the wall, suspended in time, devoid of its partner.

It wasn't the same face.

Martha's eyes were a pale shade of blue, not brown. Her chin was soft, not angular, and the flare of her nose was nothing like the girl in the mirror's. The shape of her face was different; even the hairline was different.

Oh, God. Confusion and dread spun together in her stomach like an out-of-control carnival ride. Had she gotten everything wrong? Did John and Martha have nothing at all to do with the haunting?

She backed away from the portrait slowly, her legs numb and unsteady. Her bare foot bumped against the fallen portrait on the floor, and she nearly shrieked. Pressing her lips together, she stared for a moment at the back of John's portrait. None of this made any sense. Strange things had started happening in the house after Martha died. The house hadn't even existed until they built it; no one else had lived here before them. The haunting had to be connected to the Holloways.

But then, whose face had been in the mirror?

Once she'd made it into her bedroom, she sank down on the edge of the bed. Maybe there was an explanation for the face in the mirror she hadn't thought of: maybe she was finally cracking up. She'd certainly been under a lot of stress lately. "It doesn't make any sense," she moaned, dropping her head into her hands. Her hair fell forward in ropey tendrils, dripping water onto the floor. She hadn't bothered to towel it dry in her rush to get out of the bathroom.

A heavy thud rattled the floorboards, and she sprang to her feet, clutching the towel to her hammering heart. Now what? Her eyes snapped to the doorway of the study. Something else had fallen. Or had been pushed. Would this nightmare never end?

It will end when you figure this mystery out, her inner voice insisted. *The ghost is trying to communicate. Be brave. Pretend it's your parents.*

She took a tentative step forward, trying to force her dry throat to swallow back the fear. Despite her internal pep talk, she knew it wasn't her parents. Maybe it wasn't even a relative. She inched toward the open door, goosebumps rising over every inch of her skin. That terrible chill was slithering out of the study, coiling around her. Shivers wracked her body as she peered into the room, fully expecting to find Martha's portrait missing from the wall, joined with John's to send some kind of indecipherable message.

She sucked in a breath as her eyes landed on Martha's portrait, intact and exactly where it had been a few minutes ago. Her gaze dropped to the floor, landing on a thick book beneath the shelf.

Not just a book, she realized as she moved closer. A Bible. Open to a page of handwritten notes.

Her hand rose in slow-motion to cover her mouth. She'd noticed the Bible on the shelf at some point...why hadn't she thought to look inside? Sometimes people kept family records in there; certainly a pastor would be especially likely to do that. Computer word documents and the internet had not existed during John and Martha's lifetime.

She bent forward, snatching it up as if a bony claw might shoot out from under the bookshelf and grab her wrist. The spine was worn and loose, and she made sure she marked the page it had fallen open to with her finger as she spun back toward the door. The room was so cold, she was surprised her breath didn't crystalize into puffs of smoky vapor as she fled.

Setting the Bible on the bed, she quickly changed into the warmest clothes she could find. What she'd really like was that warm bath, but no way was she going back in there right now. She hoped the whole spirit-in-the-mirror thing wouldn't affect Preston—he seemed to feel the bathroom was his safe space. At least he also liked his cat tower downstairs.

Downstairs sounded like a good idea. She didn't want to be up here. Wrapping her hair in the towel, she picked up the Bible and headed down to the kitchen, taking the back staircase from the middle landing. She poured milk into a mug, heated it the microwave, and sat back down at the kitchen table.

A cursive "Births and Deaths" headed the left page, with lines underneath for entries. A few births were listed from what appeared to be Martha's side of the family. Lark recognized some names from the family tree she'd constructed. Two daughters had been born to Martha's sister, Elizabeth; the eldest, Joan—the owner of the house before Lark—had a birth date recorded in 1930. The most recent death listed was a Holloway, so one of John's relatives. A brother, perhaps? She didn't linger over it, since it was a male name. Martha's death hadn't been recorded—John had probably been too distraught.

The right page was dedicated to "Important Dates". She studied the last two entries. "Moved into the new house—May 22, 1946". Then: "Eva arrived—October 12, 1949".

She stilled. Eva? Who the heck was Eva? Her heart thudded against her ribcage as she wracked her brain. It wasn't a baby; there hadn't been one. Unless it referred to a miscarriage or a stillbirth? Something like that belonged on the opposite side though, under births and deaths. A tingling sensation spread through her nervous system. She was onto something. She could feel it.

Who could have arrived here in October of 1949? She pulled the family tree from the pile of papers and glanced over it. No one named Eva.

The answer slammed into her, nearly taking her breath away as she rocked back in the chair. The housekeeper! There *was* someone else living here, according to what Jesse had told her last night. Someone hired in response to Martha's declining health, to help with housework and cooking. Maybe even to help care for Martha.

Despite all the terror thrown at her this evening, her feet tapped out an excited dance beneath the table. The woman in the mirror had to be Eva. Now she just needed to find out everything she could about the mystery housekeeper.

She reached for her phone, eager to text Jesse. But she paused as she thumbed the screen, remembering her plan. Keeping an emotional distance was her armor. She had to quell the instinct to immediately share things with him. She could do her own homework tonight, emailing the lawyer, the realtor...anyone who might know who Eva had been. She wasn't sure how to frame the bizarre question without sounding a bit crazy, but she'd figure it out. Then, tomorrow, she could fill Jesse in and maybe ask him to see what his mother could find out. Yes. That way, he wouldn't worry about her tonight either. She wasn't sure she would be able to say no if he invited her to his place. If that happened, she was pretty sure other stuff would happen. It would be one thing if they ended up having sex one of these days. Another thing entirely if she also started sleeping over at his house.

Somehow she had come full circle, back to Jesse. She dragged her fingers through her damp hair in an attempt to dislodge him from her brain. Then she opened up her emails and started typing.

"Are you okay?" one of the waitresses, Tatiana, asked. "You seem jumpy tonight."

That was the right word for it. When Lark had come out of the bathroom stall to find Tatiana in front of the mirrors, fixing her ponytail, Lark had startled, complete with a little "Oh!" of surprise.

"Yes, I'm fine," she assured Tatiana. *It's just that two nights ago, I saw a ghost in my own bathroom mirror, and I've been a little on edge since then.* "Just too much caffeine today," she finished out loud, which wasn't exactly true.

If she was going to be honest with herself at least, she knew it wasn't the ghost thing making her nerves sing tonight. Or at least, that wasn't the only thing.

Jesse was here, at The Boatyard, with a large group of friends. And this morning, he'd asked her to join them. When she explained she'd be there anyway, hostessing, he insisted she join them once the last of the dinner crowd had been seated.

That time had arrived—she was free to clock out. And her stomach was doing flips as she contemplated going over and sitting with the boisterous group of longtime friends.

Tatiana left as she was drying her hands, calling out for her to have a good rest of her night. Lark returned to the mirrors over the sink and checked her reflection. She was wearing a black one-piece jumpsuit, the strapless cut baring her chest and shoulders while the flowy pants covered her legs. A little sexy while still work-appropriate, she'd thought. But she didn't feel especially sexy compared to the other women in the group, who wore much clingier outfits that showed more skin. Especially the blonde, who kept reaching across the corner of the table and touching Jesse.

Lark frowned at herself. Maybe she should just take off. Claim a headache. Not that she needed a reason to bow out.

As she opened the restroom door, she did another little jump. Jesse was standing in the hallway, apparently waiting for her.

He gave her a quizzical look, combined with a killer smile. "Sorry, didn't mean to scare you."

She tucked her hair behind her ear. "No worries. It's sort of a daily occurrence for me."

His expression turned serious. "Did something else happen?"

She'd already told him about the events on Wednesday night, when she'd asked him the next morning to investigate the Eva thing. Shaking her head, she replied, "No, no. It's been quiet since Wednesday, thankfully." She twisted her fingers together. "Did you find anything out?"

"I just talked to my mom before I came here." His eyes raked over her, and he added, "You look amazing, by the way."

Her heart did a little somersault at the compliment. "Oh...thanks."

"Is this a line?" a woman asked, coming up behind them.

"Oh, no," Lark said as she moved away from the restroom doors.

"Hey, Jesse." A guy Lark recognized from the group came into the hallway. "I just bought another round," he said, jerking his thumb back in the direction of the table. "I didn't know if you wanted something different, so just go ahead and put it on my tab. I left it open."

"Thanks, Russ," Jesse said, settling a hand on her back. "This is my neighbor, Lark. She's just finishing her shift, so she's going to join us."

"Nice to meet you." Russ flashed her a smile as he moved around them toward the door to the men's room. "Feel free to add your order on. Maybe the bartender will give us an employee discount," he added with a wink.

"Why don't we go back to the table?" Jesse said under his breath. "I can fill you in on what my mom said when we have a little more privacy."

He steered her back toward the main room, his palm firmly on her back. The phrase "a little more privacy" kept echoing in her head, and her pulse skittered. How was it possible that just a small touch and a few words had such an effect on her? She needed to be careful. She hesitated, debating the headache excuse again.

"Lark? Everything okay?"

She peered up at him, unable to force out the lie. Instead, she simply said, "Maybe I should head home, and we can talk tomorrow. I really don't want to intrude on the get-together. I don't know anyone besides you."

"It's fine. I'll introduce you."

Maybe it wasn't a bad idea to meet a few more people from the area. She lifted a shoulder. "Okay. You'll have to help me remember everyone's name though. There's a lot of you."

He laughed. "Well, Russell's here for the weekend, and he hasn't seen everyone in a while. And Heather's good at getting people to come out."

"Heather?"

He gestured with his chin. "The blonde sitting near the end, wearing blue."

She didn't need to search the table. She'd already noticed the gorgeous blonde with the tight sapphire halter top. Of course it was the one who kept touching Jesse. Lark considered asking if there was something between them, now or in the past, but she bit down on her lip. What difference did it make? Jesse wasn't Lark's boyfriend. *No emotional attachments.*

He ordered a beer for himself and a glass of wine for her at the bar, which the bartender, Thomas, gave them on the house. Jesse tipped him well, then led Lark over to the group. He'd been seated at the head of the long rectangular table, and while his seat was still free, there were no other empty chairs. As soon as he brought her over and introduced her, though, the group quickly moved to accommodate her. Another chair was pulled over to squeeze in beside Jesse, and everyone shifted down a bit to create a little more space.

Lark settled into the chair, acutely aware that Heather had lost her spot near Jesse and was currently staring daggers at her. *Great*. Well, she didn't know if she'd make any new friends tonight, but she'd definitely made a new enemy.

Thankfully, there were enough people there that she didn't have to interact with Heather directly. Mostly, she just listened to their funny stories from high school. Jesse shared some fascinating stories from his time overseas, and some of the crazy things that had happened at the clinic. At some point, someone set another glass of wine down in front of her, and she drank half of it before she remembered she had to drive home.

"Whoops," she said, pushing it away.

"What is it?" asked Jesse. "Is it bad?"

"No, it's good. Too good. I was having so much fun, I forgot I still have to drive home."

The corners of his eyes crinkled as he smiled. "I'm glad you're having fun. Go ahead and finish it, and I'll drive you home." He tipped his head toward the glass of ice water in front of him. "I switched to water a while ago. And then I can fill you in on what I found out."

She pulled her hair over her shoulder, twisting it into a long coil as she pretended to think. The rational part of her brain was doing its best to shout "no!", but it was very faint, as though coming through a very bad phone connection. Too many other things were teaming up to drown it out: temptation, the wine, curiosity about Eva.

She turned to him, uncertain. "That's okay. You probably want to stay late."

He locked eyes with her, shaking his head slowly. Beneath the table, his hand settled on her thigh.

Electricity sizzled through her, stealing her breath. Oh, God. He wanted to leave his friends. To be with her. Alone. When her lungs began working again, she reached for the wine and took a healthy sip, despite not having made a decision yet on what to do. As she licked her lips, she caught him staring at her mouth. His thumb moved in a slow caress, setting her skin ablaze beneath the material of her pants.

That distant, rational part of her brain struggled to get through. "Um...wait. My car is here," she said weakly. "I have to work lunch tomorrow."

"I can run you over, no problem. I have the whole day free."

She nodded, unable to conjure any more arguments. Besides, getting a ride home with him didn't need to be a big deal. He *was* her neighbor. She *had* been drinking. And, most importantly, he had information she needed to hear, as soon as possible.

He was already starting to stage their exit, letting everyone know he was going to take off soon. Lark sipped her wine and did her best not to glance to her right, although she could feel Heather's anger rolling off of her in black waves.

As they stood up and said their goodbyes, exchanging hugs and handshakes, Lark was overwhelmed at some of the kind words and warm embraces she received. She was genuinely glad she'd stayed, and grateful for their inclusion of someone new. Crossing over to the bar, she chatted with Thomas for a moment and told him to have a good rest of his night.

She turned back toward the group, her gaze finding Jesse

down at the far end of the table. Heather had made her way down there as well, and as he took a step away, she moved in front of him, reaching up to wrap her hands around his neck. Her cropped halter lifted higher, revealing more of her tanned lower back, and Jesse's hands landed there briefly as he returned the hug. A thread of jealousy snaked its way through her, and she glanced away.

A moment later, Jesse was at her side again. "Ready?"

She nodded, trying to avoid looking in Heather's direction as Jesse reached for her hand and led them out of the restaurant. But she caught a glimpse of the other woman's lethal glare out of the corner of her eye. *None of my business*, she reminded herself. *I just need to get home safely, and to find out what Jesse knows about my resident ghost.*

Once they were outside, the getting home safely part quickly pushed its way to the forefront of her mind, mainly because Jesse was gesturing with his free hand toward his motorcycle, parked against the side of the building.

"I have my bike, but if you're not comfortable with that, I can drive your car and leave it here. I do have an extra helmet, though."

Was she comfortable with it? She'd never been on a motorcycle. But she trusted Jesse, and the ride home was only a short distance on mostly back roads. A heady frisson of excitement shivered up her spine.

"I'm game," she replied, chewing on her lip. "But I've never ridden on one before. Anything I should know in advance?"

He grinned, raking his gaze over her. "Just hold on tight and lean with me." He held up his helmet. "Here, put this on. I

have a smaller one I can use. But your hair might get a little…
wind-blown."

She smiled, lifting a shoulder. "That's what conditioner is
for." Unzipping her clutch purse, she searched for one of the
elastic ties she usually had floating around. "But I do have this,"
she added proudly as she fished one out. Handing him her
purse, she twisted her thick hair into a low ponytail as he
stowed her bag in the bike's compartment.

He settled the helmet on her head, then stepped back and
appraised her. "It looks good on you," he said, his voice low, his
tone edged with approval.

He straddled the bike, and she followed his lead, clutching
his waist as she swung her leg over to sit behind him. At his
instruction, she scooted forward, her chest pressing into the
solid muscles of his back, her inner thighs tightening around
his legs. The intimacy of the connection sent a surge of heat
through her, mixing with the balmy air caressing the bare skin
of her arms and shoulders.

The engine roared to life, vibrating beneath her, and her
heart did a wild somersault. Oh, God. "Hang on tight," he
called back to her, and then they were off, gliding out of the
parking lot, racing down the dark road.

She sensed he was taking it slow for her sake, but the sensation of flying, of the warm wind whipping by, took her breath
away. She felt…*alive*. This wasn't something she could ever
imagine being able to do in New York City. She savored the
solid strength of his body, the vast expanse of open skies and
quiet roads, and the fresh scent of the night air as she clung
to him.

Too soon, they were turning down the road to their houses, and he called out, "My house okay? I should probably let the dogs out."

She craned forward to bring her mouth next to his ear. "Yes, that's fine." She definitely didn't want to discuss anything related to the haunting at her house. Too many weird things seemed to happen when she made comments out loud.

The dogs appeared in the window as they pulled into his driveway, and a smile tugged at her lips. She loved Preston, but it would be nice to have this kind of welcome home any time she arrived. Jesse cut the engine, and she reluctantly released her iron grip on him.

He helped her off and retrieved her bag, stowing the helmets. "What did you think?"

"I loved it," she replied, her smile growing wider as he flashed her a grin.

"Excellent. Maybe we can go for another ride this weekend. Head up to Provincetown or something. Have you been yet?"

She shook her head, following him toward the house. Bosco's excited barking rang out through the open windows, and as they passed, the dogs scrambled off the couch to head to the door.

She couldn't bring herself to say anything more about a trip to Provincetown with him. That sounded like a date—an amazing date—but she needed to be careful. This was going to come down to a delicate balance between what her mind dictated and what her body craved.

An image of Nathan and Brittney flashed through her mind, and her stomach clenched. Before she could stop herself, she blurted out, "So, what's the deal with that Heather girl?" Even to her own ears, the question sounded childish and insecure, and she regretted it immediately. But it was out there now, and she needed to know.

He paused, his hand on the doorknob. Beneath the glow of the outdoor light, his handsome features hardened with concern as he met her gaze. "Heather? Did she do something?" His eyes narrowed, a muscle twitching along his jaw.

"No, not exactly. I just got a weird vibe from her." *If looks could kill, I'd be lying dead on the floor of The Boatyard*, her inner voice added grimly.

"Ah." He opened the door and ushered her inside as the dogs greeted them both enthusiastically. Once the initial chaos had calmed, he motioned her toward the kitchen. "I'm sorry if she made you uncomfortable. She's my ex, but it's been over for a long time."

"Does she know that?"

He laughed, sliding open the back door to let the dogs into the yard. He closed the screen and turned back to her. "She knows. I've been very clear. We dated in high school, and off and on when I was in college, but it's been years since then. She's just...used to getting what she wants."

"And she wants you."

Sighing, he shrugged. "I think she just wants what she can't have." He opened the fridge door and pulled out a beer. "Want something? Another glass of wine? Water? Warm milk?" he added with a wink that made it clear he was more referencing an inside joke than teasing her.

Her taut muscles relaxed a few degrees, and she struggled

to rein in the jealousy clawing at her. What in the world was she doing? Jealousy was an emotion, and that did not fit in with her "no emotional attachments" rule. A change of subject was needed. They should discuss the info she was here for, and then she should get home.

"Lark?" he asked, still poised by the open fridge, brows raised.

"Oh, um…" What the hell. Maybe more wine would help her chase these unwanted thoughts away. "Sure, I'll have a small glass of wine. If you have it."

"I do." He retrieved a wine glass from a cabinet and poured her a glass of white. She filled a water glass at the sink and downed some of that first as he let the dogs back in.

"So…what did your mom have to say?" she asked, leaning back against the island. A sudden memory of him pressing her back against the edge of this counter—while kissing her senseless—surfaced, and she fought to keep the flush from her cheeks.

"Well, she found out a few things, although I'm not sure how helpful it will be. She did confirm that Eva was the person hired to help Martha."

Her pulse jumped. "Really? Oh, that's very helpful. At least we know that now." Neither the lawyer nor the realtor had been able to give her any information on a woman named Eva who may have lived with the Holloways in the 1950s.

"True. How she got here is interesting, anyway. She wasn't exactly hired. She was a Polish World War II refugee, living in a displaced persons camp in Europe. She lost her family and home in the war."

"Oh, that's so sad."

He nodded, his face grim, and she remembered he'd seen the death and devastation of war firsthand. Her chest tightened. Life was already filled with so much tragedy and heartbreak...why did human beings have to inflict it on each other?

Taking a swig from the beer bottle, he continued. "Apparently, the United States passed a Displaced Persons Act in the summer of 1948, allowing some of the European refugees to settle in America. There were some requirements, like the refugee had to have a sponsor here and a place to live. Religious organizations helped set things up, and Pastor John's church was involved in the effort."

"Wow. So she came over here by herself?"

"From what my mother's friends said, she was technically an adult, but young...18 or 19. John and Martha were her sponsors, and they offered her a place to live in exchange for helping with housework, helping care for Martha, and possibly one day helping with the children they hoped to have."

Her mind swirled, trying to fit this new information into the puzzle. Unfortunately, the puzzle still didn't have much structure. Just a bunch of scattered pieces lying around, refusing to connect. She scrunched her mouth, turning the stem of the wineglass in her fingers.

He read her thoughts. "I'm not sure if any of that is helpful in terms of solving the mystery. Because then Martha died, so no one needed to take care of her, and there wouldn't be any children. It wouldn't have been appropriate for a young unmarried woman to stay and live alone with a widower, so she was sent to a family in Boston."

She raised her gaze to his, their eyes locking. "I wonder if there's any way to verify that."

"The same thought occurred to me, but we don't have a last name. My mom's friends couldn't remember it, so it's going to be difficult to track her down. I did a quick online search and looked up how many people came over as part of the Displaced Persons Act, and it's not a small number. Over 400,000. First we'd have to find her individual info, maybe by using the date you found in the Bible, but I'm not sure the records would include anything beyond where a refugee was first placed. Also, from what I read, those records aren't accessible online. They seem to be in storage in D.C."

She sighed, combing her hand through her hair. "Great. Well, I doubt the records would be all that useful, anyway. If she died in some tragedy, it probably wouldn't be documented in those records. Either something happened in that house, or somewhere else, but her spirit returned to the house. If the ghost is Eva, that is." She lifted a shoulder. "But I think it must be."

His jaw tightened. "I wish I had something more for you."

Her hair swung against her back as she shook her head vehemently. "No, what your mom was able to find is amazing. Please tell her and her friends how much I appreciate it. Thank you, too. I know this isn't your problem."

He closed the distance between them, setting his beer on the island. "I hate thinking about you all alone in that house."

"Then don't think about it," she said, her tone light with the attempted joke. Her small smile faded when he didn't return it.

The proximity of his body made her nerves tingle with awareness.

His eyes darkened as he looked down at her. "That might be tough. I find myself thinking about you all the time."

"You do?" The words came out in a husky whisper, and she swallowed.

Instead of answering, he grazed his knuckle across her cheek, trailing a streak of heat.

Her breath caught. Held.

He bent his head, capturing her lips in a series of lingering kisses, each one a smoldering connection that made her desperate for more. Moaning, she leaned into him, sliding her palms up his muscled chest. His kisses moved to the corner of her mouth, along her jaw, down the tender flesh of her neck. *Oh, God.* She gasped as shivers shot through her like fireworks.

His tongue ran along her collarbone, his fingers slipping beneath the elastic band of her strapless top. She locked her arms around his neck, pressing her hips into his, savoring the feel of his arousal. *She did that to him.* He wanted her. She wanted him. Nothing else mattered.

The world disappeared, conscious thought receding as need took over. She arched her back as his hand slid over her breast, her knees going weak as the rough pads of his fingers brushed across her taut nipples. She pushed her thigh between his legs, and he groaned.

"Bedroom," he said thickly, the word somewhere between a question and a statement. He caught her mouth in another all-consuming kiss, leaving her unable to answer. Or even to think. Every cell in her body ached for him. She managed a breathless sound of assent, and he began pulling her toward the stairs.

He tugged her through his bedroom door, then shut it behind them before the dogs could follow them any farther. Walking her backwards, he pressed her against the door, his arms caging her in as he kissed her ravenously. She wrapped her hands around the hard muscles of his neck, lifting to her toes to get closer. She met his kisses with a matching urgency, only pulling away to drag his shirt over his head. Their mouths clashed again, tongues exploring as he ran his palms over her arms. He hooked his thumbs into the elastic band of her top and dragged it down, following the material with his lips, over her breasts, down her stomach, to the lace edge of her black panties. Her outfit puddled to the floor, and he kneeled in front of her, his hands fanned over her hips, his warm breath caressing the sensitive skin of her belly. She dug her nails into his shoulders, every nerve quivering with anticipation. The moment stretched out with agonizing deliberation, the slow intensity heightening the feverish passion like the calm before the storm. Her heart banged against her ribcage, the sound echoing in her ears. The lace thong inched down her thighs, along her calves, over her ankles, each brush of his fingers against her flesh tormenting her, building an unbearable pressure deep within her. She whimpered, pulling at him, needing his body against hers again.

He rose, lifting her up, once more pinning her to the door. Her shoulder blades ground against the wood as she clung to him, wrapping her legs around his waist. She sought his mouth, reveling in the taste of him, desperate to get her fill. Heat surged through her, raging like wildfire.

He carried her toward the bed, his strong arms supporting her weight, his lips never leaving hers. Hurry. She needed all of him. Now. Her body craved release; she was going to go mad without it.

He laid her down, unbuttoning his shorts in one swift motion, and she tugged at the layers of clothing with him. Silvery moonlight filtered in through the open windows, accentuating the definition of his chest and shoulders, the hard planes and sculpted muscles. Their eyes met, his dark with desire, and the seconds spooled out, measured in heartbeats. Realization suddenly flashed across his face, and he blinked. "Condom," he said roughly, shifting his weight.

"I'm on the pill," she said, the words rushing out. She hadn't stopped taking it. And maybe the prudent thing would be to use one anyway, but right now, her mind was a dull haze. She had been reduced to raw nerves and smoldering flesh, and all she wanted was to feel Jesse inside her, no barriers between them.

"You're sure?" he murmured, bending his head to nuzzle her neck. He moved lower, his mouth closing over her nipple as his fingers stroked between her thighs.

A raspy sound of assent was the best she could do as powerful sensations washed over her. When she remembered how to speak, she managed, "Yes. I'm sure." Her voice was strained with need, her hips lifting, legs trembling. *Please. Hurry.*

He pushed himself into her with delicious deliberation,

slow and controlled, until she was filled with his hard heat. With a groan, he thrust deeper, and a gasp tore from her throat.

"Am I hurting you?"

She shook her head wordlessly, gripping his back, rocking her hips beneath him. He matched her rhythm, driving into her, sending waves of pleasure crashing through her. Oh, God. Yes. The waves built into a crescendo, and she shattered, crying out. His lips caught her whimpers, his fingers knotting in her hair as he came over the edge with her. Aftershocks shuddered through her, and he touched his forehead to hers, their ragged breaths mingling in the darkness.

"Lark," he murmured, scraping the scruff of his jaw across her cheek. He sank onto her, the solid weight of his body holding her captive. She ran her hands along his back, her palms sliding over slick skin and hard ridges. As her heartrate slowed, her limbs grew heavy, and she drifted, still awash in sensations. He rolled to his side, pulling her with him, gathering her in his arms and settling the comforter over their entwined bodies in one intimate motion that made her chest contract. He held her tightly, his fingers brushing her temple as his breathing evened.

This was bliss, and she didn't want it to end. When sleep reached up to claim her, she slipped seamlessly into its comforting depths.

13

*H*er shoulders sagged as she checked her phone again. Why wasn't Nathan answering? She dropped the phone back into her bag and dug out her keyring. Sliding the key into the lock, she let herself into his apartment.

Had Nathan known? Was his job safe? She blew out a frustrated breath. For all she knew, he could currently be packing his office belongings into cardboard boxes as human resources waited to escort him out. She grimaced, setting down her own solitary box—all she'd needed for her picture frames and coffee cups—onto the floor. *God.* Maybe that's why he wasn't answering his phone. If he was also getting laid off, they were in serious trouble.

A muffled moan drifted through the apartment, and she froze, her eyes snapping to the closed bedroom door. What the hell? Bedsprings squeaked in time with a rhythmic thumping. Her stomach clenched, some primal part of her understanding what she was hearing before her already battered brain could interpret the sounds. Her vision swam, the edges of the front room blurring as she reached out and put a hand against the wall.

Someone was having sex in there. But this was Nathan's apartment, and he lived alone...and he was presumably at work. Even if he was home, she was his fiancé, and she was standing right here. She glanced over at her splayed fingers as if checking the diamond ring for confirmation.

It must be someone else. She nodded to herself, swallowing down the nausea bubbling up like rancid oil. Then a louder noise—a familiar groan.

That was Nathan.

She'd just gotten fired, and her fiancé was having sex with someone else in the bed she regularly shared with him? This was too much.

Anger burned through her, sharp and blinding. She stalked over to the bedroom, steeling herself as she gripped the knob. Then she opened the door.

She jolted awake, her heart racing, eyes peering through the darkness at the unfamiliar surroundings. A heavy arm draped across her middle quickly brought her back to reality. Jesse. She was in his room, not at Nathan's apartment in the city. The dream faded as consciousness seeped back in, but the ugly images remained, playing out in her head. That scene, unfortunately, hadn't originated in a dream. It just revisited her there, a painful reminder of everything that had happened. Of why she was here, on Cape Cod.

Her pulse continued to surge, and a clammy sweat broke

out over her skin. A vise tightened around her chest, strangling her breaths. *I need to get out of here.*

This had been a mistake. Not the sex—there was no denying that had been amazing. But staying over with him, sleeping here. That's what couples did. Sleeping beside him felt safe. Comfortable. Comforting. And that was dangerous. Certainly not the way to avoid an emotional attachment. Her subconscious was trying to warn her. And now her body was following suit with some kind of panic attack.

Despite the urge to tear herself away from him, she slowly slipped from under his arm, praying he would not wake up. Bosco glanced up at her from the end of the bed. She dimly remembered Jesse getting up at some point to get his cell phone, in case of a vet emergency, and the dogs coming in. Please be quiet, she begged them silently. Benny offered her a soft snore from the floor beside the bed in answer.

She crept over to the door, bending down to gather her clothes. She'd lost her sandals somewhere downstairs before they'd made their way up. She quickly dressed in the hallway, fighting against the dizziness threatening to pull her under. Her legs trembled as she tiptoed down the stairs.

She located her sandals in the kitchen, and she slipped them on, trying not to think about how they came to be strewn across the floor in the first place, kicked off as she and Jesse fumbled and groped their way to the stairs. And she certainly didn't want to think about what came after. Not right now, or she might lose her courage.

Her car was still at The Boatyard. No big deal, she could walk home. It was the middle of the night, but her bag with her phone was sitting on the island. She grabbed it and turned toward the front door, then hesitated.

He'd be worried if he woke up and found her gone. That was the kind of guy he was. She searched the shadows of the kitchen counters, finally spotting a pad of paper and a pen. Moving as quietly as possible, she carried them over to the island so she could leave a note.

But what could she write? She tapped the end of the pen against her lips, still tender from Jesse's ravenous kisses. God, she was so close to falling for him. She needed to pull herself back from the edge before she tumbled headfirst, exposing her heart to more pain.

She couldn't write that. It was too hard to explain, and it sounded presumptuous, anyway. Just because she was in danger of developing deep feelings for him didn't mean he was in the same place. She was pretty sure he'd share her view that the sex had been mind-blowingly incredible. But he might not understand that despite how close they'd been, waking up together was just too intimate for her to bear. It felt like assigning a significance to what had happened. Placing it further away from just sex and closer to relationship territory.

Hurry up. Just write something truthful and to-the-point. She touched the tip of the pen to the paper and scribbled, "I had to get home. Didn't want to wake you." There. She resisted the urge to add, "Everything's fine," because everything was *not* fine. Her heart was still flailing about, as though trying to escape from her ribcage. Fresh waves of betrayal surged through her, leaking out of the ragged wound the dream had torn open. Her head hurt from the wine and the ramifications of what she'd done. Hopefully Jesse would just be glad she was gone and no excuses would be necessary to get her out of his house so he could have a peaceful morning alone.

She'd go out the front door, so she could lock it behind her. She crept through the dark, silent house like a thief, cringing at every tiny sound she made. Then she let herself out into the night.

14

He stared at the note on the kitchen island, his brows pulling together. He hadn't been expecting that. He'd been expecting her. When he'd awoken, he'd already been reaching for her, seeking to pull her back into his arms. And, yeah, his body had been aching for her again, arousal pulling him out of his dreams.

Disappointment had rushed through him when he realized she wasn't still in bed, but he expected to find her somewhere in the house. The kitchen seemed the logical place. Not that there was much to offer there, but the rack next to his coffee machine was always stocked with pods of both coffee and tea, and there was orange juice in the fridge and fruit in the bowl by her note.

The dogs whined, and he let them out back, staring for a moment at the woods blocking the view of her house. What time had she left? He'd come downstairs to get his phone around 12:30, relieved to find no missed calls that might indicate an emergency, and she'd still been in bed when he returned. Maybe she just woke up really early and wanted to go home and get changed. She had to work the lunch shift—maybe she needed to get some things done before she went in.

He checked the time on his phone: 7:45 a.m. He'd need to drive her to work, as promised. Maybe tonight he could take her to dinner in Provincetown, like he mentioned. She might be from a busy city, but he felt reasonably certain she'd never seen anything like Ptown on a Saturday night in the summertime. Just watching the parade of people along Commercial Street was entertainment, and then there were all the restaurants, art galleries, and shops.

After he brewed coffee, he took his mug outside and sat on the patio. Pulling out his phone, he brought up their text chain and typed, "Hey. I missed you this morning. Everything OK?"

By the time she answered, an hour had passed, and he was headed out the door to the gym. He frowned as he read her response. "All OK. One of the waitresses is picking me up on her way to work, so you don't need to worry about giving me a ride."

Something about the tone of the text bothered him, but then again, it was a text. He typed back, asking if she wanted to head to Ptown for dinner after her shift.

Dots appeared, then disappeared. He shook his head, closing the door behind him and straddling his bike. As he pulled on his helmet, a chime sounded, and he dug his phone back out.

"Think I'll probably be tired after working last night and today. But thanks anyway."

He jammed the phone back into the compartment of his bike, along with his gym stuff. Something was clearly wrong. Did she regret last night? There was no doubt in his mind she'd wanted him just as much as he wanted her.

Her questions about Heather surfaced in his mind as he started up the engine. Hopefully that wasn't giving Lark second thoughts.

Second thoughts about what? Why was he even thinking this way? They'd had phenomenal sex last night, but she was still hell-bent on leaving town as soon as she could sell the house. He was helping her solve the mystery that might make it happen faster. Sure, his protective nature also wanted to keep her safe, but she had told him more than once she preferred to rely on herself.

That was fine. If she needed space, she could take it. If she wanted to see him, she knew where he lived. If something scary happened and she needed him, she had his number.

Until then, he was going to put her out of his mind. Clenching his jaw, he leaned in to take the turn, then opened up and sped down the road, letting the roar of the engine drown out his thoughts.

BY SUNDAY NIGHT, she estimated she had checked her phone at least a hundred times over the remainder of the weekend, simultaneously hoping Jesse had texted her, and hoping he hadn't. This obsessive behavior was exactly the reason she'd been right to put some distance between them. She couldn't stop thinking about him. And if she managed, even for a few seconds, her body would remind her with twinges of delicious soreness from every sensitive spot she had. Damn it to hell.

She'd even taken herself to Provincetown for the day, to get out of the house, and get him out of her mind. She had to admit, it was a wild place, even on a Sunday afternoon. But she just kept wishing he was with her.

The best part of her day had been exploring the galleries and talking to the artists and photographers about their work. There was everything ranging from large studios filled with the work of one incredibly talented photographer, to small collective shops selling the work of multiple artists and crafters. She'd even been given a card for a collective looking for someone else to join the group. Everyone split the rent, displayed their work, and contributed hours working in the shop. Of course, she was rusty, not to mention the fact that she probably wouldn't be around for the entire summer...but still, it was nice to be asked.

Maybe they'd like a nice ghost photo, she thought to herself as she poured soup into a saucepan. She could frame them all; offer up an entire series: "Eva, the Spirit of Holloway House". Or, as an alternative title, "The Reason I'm Now Terrified to Look in the Bathroom Mirror". A wry grimace pulled at her lips. Tourists were probably seeking something more along the lines of her shots of the beach.

She'd brought her camera with her and taken dozens of photographs in the few hours she'd been there. She'd have to take a look after dinner and see if anything came out decent.

Hopefully no wayward phantoms had made their way into these pictures.

Stirring the soup, she reached for her phone yet again. Nothing from Jesse. A melancholy ache settled in her chest. What did she expect, after the way she'd shut him down? Lord, she was a mess.

As she closed her messages, a notification from her calendar popped up, and her pulse skittered. A reminder about Preston's follow-up vet appointment. Tomorrow morning.

She sighed, slapping her phone down on the counter and twisting off the burner. So much for distance. But she had to go—what choice did she have?

This wouldn't be awkward at all.

_____

15

*L*ark set the cat carrier onto the floor of the empty exam room and opened the metal door. Despite all the howling Preston did on the way to the vet's office, now that he was free to climb out of the carrier, he didn't budge. She didn't blame him. She wished she could crawl in there with him, to be honest.

She fidgeted beside the metal exam table, glancing repeatedly at the far door as she struggled against the anxiety coursing through her veins. Beads of sweat collected along her hairline, and she swiped an arm across her forehead. Just getting dressed for this appointment had taken an inordinate amount of thought and energy. Ridiculous.

The door leading to the back of the clinic opened, and Jesse strode in. He gave her a tight smile that didn't reach his eyes. "How's he doing?" he asked, getting right to business.

"Oh…ah…I think he's doing well. Although he doesn't want to come out." She gestured toward the carrier on the floor.

Jesse picked it up by the sides and gently tipped it until Preston spilled out onto the table. "Hey, buddy," he murmured to the cat, corralling him before he could jump off and escape back into the carrier. He palpitated Preston's belly, not looking at Lark. "Is he eating okay?"

"Yes. He's eating the special food, and he's been using the litterbox."

"Good." With one hand, he hooked the stethoscope around his neck into his ears, then maneuvered the silver chest piece onto Preston's fur.

The room was quiet as he listened, and the tension seemed to expand in the silence. She couldn't take it anymore. "How was the rest of your weekend?"

He glanced up at her, removing the ear pieces and wrapping the stethoscope back around his neck. "Uneventful."

She chewed on her lower lip. It didn't seem like a good idea to discuss how she'd taken it upon herself to visit Province-town after declining his invitation. But she could at least share that the ghost had been quiet, thankfully. "Mine, too," she offered, even though he didn't ask. "No paranormal activity, although at this point I still just sleep on the couch."

His eyes flashed, and she realized her mistake. She'd hoped to resurrect the couch joke, but on Friday night, she'd slept in a bed. His bed, to be specific. Until she'd snuck out, leaving an impersonal note like the coward she was.

"Glad to hear it," he said tersely, peering into Preston's eyes. "He seems to be doing fine."

"Listen…" she trailed off, swallowing hard. "Friday night was…well, it was amazing."

He met her gaze, brows raised. "Sounds like there's a 'but' coming." He released Preston, and the cat jumped lightly to the exam room floor and scurried back into his carrier.

"No, no 'but'. It's just that…I'm not going to be staying here, so I don't think we should start anything. You know?"

His shoulder lifted. "You've been very upfront about your plans to leave. I suppose I just didn't see any issue with us dating while you were here."

Oh, God, she was really messing this up. She twisted her fingers together, shifting her weight. "I think the issue is…we could get too close."

He nodded. "Got it." Turning his back on her, he washed his hands at the sink. "I have to get to my next client, Lark." His voice was firm and businesslike, edged with steel.

"Oh, of course," she said miserably. What was she thinking, bringing all this up while he was at work? "We're all set, then?" She swept her hand toward the carrier to indicate she was referring to the cat. She already knew she and Jesse were all set. Over. Done.

"Yes. Everything looks good. But he may always be susceptible to another blockage, so you should keep him on the special diet and stay alert for any future issues."

"I will."

He gave her a brisk nod. "Take care," he said as he turned to leave, a hard undercurrent of finality in his tone.

She watched the door close behind him, her vision swimming as something inside her broke.

16

A canine whine registered first, breaking through layers of sleep. Jesse stirred, rolling to his side. Then a frantic cry ripped through the darkness, and he tensed, his eyes snapping open. Bosco leapt off the bed and charged to the open window, propping himself up on the ledge.

"Help!"

Jesse was on his feet in seconds. Lark! He recognized her voice, but he also recognized the sobbing pleas for help. A jolt of alarm surged through him as scenes from the last time he'd heard her screams echoing through the night played out in his mind. The unseen pursuer, her eerie struggle, the collapse of her body beside the river.

"Help me!"

He raced down the stairs and into the kitchen, both dogs at his heels now. He wasn't wearing anything but boxer briefs, but he wasn't about to take the time to put more clothes on. Pushing the dogs back with his bare foot, he hauled open the slider, then slammed it shut firmly behind him. He was running before he'd even turned away from the house, his long strides carrying him across the yard, his pulse pounding in time with his feet. He crossed the yard quickly, catching sight of her as he neared the woods. She stumbled through the trees, terror etched in every movement, sinking to her knees by the bank of the river. "No, please," she moaned.

"Lark!" he yelled, hoping somehow his voice might break the spell. "Wake up!" He pushed himself harder, summoning a burst of speed as he crossed the bridge. He watched in horror as her body toppled forward, her hair falling over her face as her head dropped out of view.

Damn it! A series of splashes revealed at least some part of her had hit the water. He had no flashlight, but the moon was nearly full, its glow filtering through branches to dimly define the shadows. The pale skin of her bare legs flashed in the darkness as she kicked wildly at the forest floor.

As he closed the last stretch of distance between them, his stomach lurched at the angle of her body—chest folded over the bank, head dangling, her hands flailing at the surface of the water. Her lower body writhed and fought for leverage, as though someone were holding her down.

This time, he was sure someone *was* holding her down. He didn't understand how, but he knew it was no dream. Not a regular dream, anyway.

Icy air surrounded his arms as he grabbed her around the waist. He hauled her up and back, wrenching her away from the unseen force. A numb, prickling sensation washed over his flesh, and corresponding nausea churned in his stomach.

The air around them was cold and dense, inhabited by a tangle of pain and terror. He clutched her to him, her body limp against his chest, and pulled her farther away from the river.

He laid her down on the ground, kneeling beside her, and she thrashed weakly, moaning. Beneath her closed lids, her eyes fluttered, and strands of wet hair stuck to her pale cheeks. Cradling the sides of her head, he brought his face close to hers. "Lark. Wake up, baby." Please. "It's okay. You're okay."

Her chest shuddered as she sucked in a breath, releasing it on a spasm of coughs. Her eyes dragged open, and she stared blankly at him.

"Lark?" A thread of relief snaked through him, but adrenaline continued to pour into his veins like jolts of electricity. She appeared awake, now, although he didn't believe she'd exactly been asleep. More like in a trance, under a spell, cast by whatever was in that house. He prayed his voice could break it. "I'm here, baby. I've got you."

She groaned, her lax expression beginning to sharpen as her eyes focused. "Jesse?" Her gaze moved from his as she took in their surroundings. Comprehension slowly overtook confusion, but the fear remained etched across her face. "Oh, no," she murmured, craning her neck to lift her head off the ground. "It happened again."

"Yeah," he answered softly, reaching for her hand. He rubbed his palms over her chilled flesh. "But you're okay now."

Lifting her free arm, she touched the sodden stands of hair plastered to her neck, her eyes seeking his with an unspoken question.

"You were on the river bank again. This time you nearly fell in." *Were nearly pushed in*, his inner voice growled.

She blinked slowly, heaving a sigh. "Someone was chasing me. In the dream, or whatever. But…it wasn't me. *I* wasn't me." She rubbed her forehead. "Sorry, I know that doesn't make sense."

"Don't apologize. I want you to try to explain it. But first, I need to know if you're hurt."

"My head hurts. Not like I bumped it or anything. Inside. Like a headache, but…different."

He frowned. "You're freezing, too. I need to get you inside. Get you warmed up."

She nodded, the back of her head rustling against the pine needles and leaves. "Yes. Okay."

He slid his arm beneath her upper back and helped her to sit up. "Can you walk?"

Nodding again, she let him help her to her feet. Once again, she was barely dressed, clad only in a long T-shirt. *His* T-shirt, he suddenly realized, his heart tightening.

If he had anything on, he'd give her extra layers to warm her up. He settled for tucking her under his shoulder, enfolding her in his arms and sharing his body heat. He led them toward the bridge, and she huddled beside him, not protesting as he helped her up the hill toward his house. An owl hooted in the darkness, the repetitive calls an unnerving accompaniment to their silent trek.

He took them in through the unlocked slider, pushing the dogs away and hustling her to the couch. Spreading a blanket over her, he ran upstairs and grabbed a sweatshirt for her, pulling on his own clothes as he made his way back down. He quickly heated a mug of milk, his thoughts spinning along with the microwave turntable.

What was he going to do? She'd made her feelings clear over the weekend—and reiterated her stance a few days ago at Preston's appointment. She didn't want to be with him. But there was simply no way he could let her go back home after this. It was too dangerous, and this was now the second time it had happened. The first time, they'd been able to chalk it up to some sort of sleepwalking incident. Now they knew they were dealing with a frightening supernatural entity. They even had images on film.

Carrying the warm drink to her, he placed it in her hands and sat down across from her. He raked his gaze over her, but she was almost entirely covered by the blanket and draped with two dogs. The scene was so reminiscent of the last time, it felt like they'd been thrust into the past. He dragged a hand over his jaw, the rough stubble reminding him how late it was. A thread of unease twisted in his gut as he glanced at the clock on the wall. The timeframe of the two incidents was the same as well—it was now nearly 1:30 a.m., which meant he'd found her by the river a little after 1:00. Just like before.

He dropped his hand, rubbing his palms on the sweatpants he'd thrown on. "Lark. Are you okay? You sure you're not injured?"

She sipped at her drink, her hands wrapped around the mug's warmth. "I don't know about okay, but I'm not injured." A tremor traveled through her, and she averted her gaze.

"Look. I know you don't want my help. But you can't go

back to that house tonight." He pressed his lips together, then plunged ahead. "You need to stay here. In one of the guest rooms. I promise I won't touch you, so you don't need to worry about that."

Her face crumpled, and she dropped her head. Benny lifted his nose toward her, sensing some shift in emotions. A long hiccupping breath tore from her chest, an opening of the floodgates. Then suddenly she was sobbing, one hand covering her mouth in an attempt to muffle the choked gasps.

Christ. What was happening? He watched in horror as her body shook, tears dripping to the blanket. Bosco whined, unsettled. The dog looked at him, as if urging him to do something. He hesitated for a moment, unsure whether he should now touch her after just promising he wouldn't. But instinct took over, and he hurried to her, nudging Bosco aside as he dropped to the couch beside her, enfolding her in his arms.

"Hey. It's going to be okay. We'll try to find a hotel room if that's what you need." That wouldn't be easy, in the middle of the night in summertime on Cape Cod. But he might be able to pull some strings if he had to. Or maybe Diane would let her stay over. "I just want to make sure you're safe."

Something he said triggered a worse onslaught of wracking sobs, and her chest heaved as she fought to catch her breath. He held her silently, his teeth clenching against the feeling of helplessness. Warm tears drenched his neck, ripping holes in his heart.

When her weeping tapered off, she lifted her head, shaking it slowly. "Sorry," she murmured, her voice ragged. She sniffled, wiping at her face with trembling fingers.

"It's fine. Hang on, I'll grab you some tissues." He rose, nearly sprinting to the bathroom and returning with the box. "Here." He gently set the box on her lap and sat back down, rubbing his palm over her back as she swiped at her eyes and nose.

He gave her time, going over their brief conversation in his head, searching for what had set her off. Something he'd said? Or just fear and exhaustion? He had the feeling there was something even deeper going on here, but whether she would confide in him was anyone's guess.

When she met his gaze again, her eyes were red and swollen, filled with anguish. "I don't usually get hysterical like that."

"I'd say, under the circumstances, most people would."

She nodded, twisting the sodden tissue in her hands. "Having no control like that...your body being directed by someone else. By *something* else. It's scary."

"Downright terrifying, I'd guess."

"But it's not that. Or not *just* that." She swallowed audibly. "It's what you said, about promising not to touch me."

He tensed, the motion of his hand against her back coming to an abrupt halt.

"That's not what I want," she said breathlessly, the words rushing out like a confession. "I don't want you to never touch me again."

Confusion knotted his muscles. He had no idea how to respond, and a heavy silence hung in the air for a few beats.

"I know it's my fault, but it hurt me to hear you say that. It's not what I want. But there's a reason I felt like that's the way it had to be." She hung her head, her damp hair falling forward. "I owe you an explanation."

What was going on? He gave her shoulder a gentle squeeze before dropping his arm away. "You don't owe me anything, Lark."

She peered up at him, her features set with determination. "I want to tell you why I ran away the other night."

17

*S*he *did* owe him the truth about why she'd left like that. But the idea of revealing what had happened, the thought of sharing that betrayal, made her stomach clench into a tight fist. Pulling a fresh tissue from the box, she dabbed at her swollen eyes, suddenly picturing what she must look like. She'd gone from fast asleep, to staggering through the woods, to dunking her head into a river, to prolonged hysterical crying…not a great combination.

Gathering the used tissues, she shifted forward on the couch. "Okay if I run to the bathroom and splash some water on my face first?"

"Of course," he answered, pushing himself up to standing and lifting her mug off the table. "Want a refill?"

"Um…sure." She followed him toward the kitchen, tossing the tissues into the trash can as he pointed out the downstairs bathroom. "Actually, maybe something stronger, if you have it."

"I was going to pour a whisky myself. Too strong?" He held

up an expensive-looking bottle he'd pulled from a lower cabinet.

"Not for this night. I think I could use it." Her gaze fell on the oven clock as she turned toward the bathroom, and a sudden realization crashed over her. "Oh my God! It's almost 2:00 in the morning, and you have to work tomorrow!" She dragged her fingers through her tangled hair. "I am so sorry. I should go."

"You're not going back to that house tonight. Remember?"

She sucked in a breath at the mention of the house, steadying herself in the doorway as her legs wobbled. "Oh, no —what about Preston? Last time I did this, I left the front door of the house wide open. But he's not locked in the upstairs bathroom tonight."

He set down the two low-ball glasses and crossed toward the slider. "I'll go right now and make sure he's still inside, and lock up. Do you need anything?"

She couldn't think straight. "But...you need to go to sleep. It's a weeknight," she added dully, as if he didn't know.

"I'll be fine. I've gone many nights with no sleep over the years. I'm going to run over and check on the house, and then we're going to talk. Okay?" His voice held no room for argument, and his gaze remained locked on hers as he waited for an answer.

"Yes. Okay." She started to close the bathroom door, then added, "Hurry back. And please be careful."

When she met her reflection in the mirror, she almost wished a phantom face had taken its place. Good Lord. Bending over, she splashed cold water on her face, wishing she had a brush and some concealer. Oh well, what did it matter? She was going to tell him her story, expose her shattered self-worth, and then let him get to bed. Still, she did her best to fix her appearance as she waited for him to return. As she adjusted the enormous sweatshirt he'd lent her, she suddenly realized she was wearing his T-shirt underneath. Since Monday's heartbreak, she'd been sleeping in it, unable to deny herself the security it provided, even if it came with pain. Had he noticed? Oh, God, she was pathetic.

In the kitchen, she rinsed out her mug, staring anxiously out the window into the inky blackness. Was he okay? Was Preston okay? Searching for something else to do, she picked up the bottle of whisky on the counter and poured a healthy amount into each glass. The sharp, smoky tang filled her nostrils as she raised the glass to her lips, and she took a tentative sip. With a grimace, she swallowed, the fiery liquid burning a path down her throat and into her belly. Whoa.

The sliding door opened, and she whirled around, eyes wide with her questions and the sting of the alcohol.

"Preston's inside," Jesse assured her, closing the door. "I found him in his bed in the upstairs bathroom."

Relief sluiced through her, and she sagged against the counter. Benny's tail thumped against the kitchen floor, as if he was also pleased to hear the news.

Jesse strode over and held out a pink polka-dotted toiletries bag. "I didn't know what you might need, so I found this under the sink and just threw everything from the counter that would fit inside."

"Oh, thank you. For everything." She accepted the bag

gratefully, making a quick mental inventory of what she had left lying around the sink. Anything embarrassing? Her birth control pills. But he knew about that already. A warm flush crept up her neck as memories of that night flashed through her mind, and she took another swig of the whisky. Putting the bag down, she handed him the other glass she'd poured.

"Everything's locked up over there, and I put a key from the hook beside the door in the bag," he said, glancing down at the amber liquid as he swirled it around. "If you're ready, I'd like to hear what you wanted to tell me."

"You're sure? I know it's late."

"I'm sure," he said firmly, tipping his chin toward the living room. The dogs followed them as they made their way out of the kitchen.

She returned to her spot on the couch, and he sat down in the chair across from her. Bosco jumped up beside her, settling his heavy head on her lap, as if realizing she needed support. Benny turned a few circles and sank down onto the floor beside Jesse.

She hesitated, uncertain how to begin, and even more uncertain she was ready to share this story. Thinking about it was painful enough; talking about it would scrape her insides raw. But maybe she needed to let it out. Aside from Madison, she hadn't told a soul. Maybe it would be cathartic…a way to release the inner demons haunting her heart, since she couldn't seem to vanquish the ones haunting her home.

Pulling in a calming breath, she plunged ahead, not wanting to keep him up any later with her procrastination. "About a year and a half ago, my parents went to Hawaii for their anniversary. It was their dream trip." A sad smile tugged at her lips, then fell away. "But there was a car accident, and it was... fatal. They both died."

"Oh, Lark...I'm so sorry."

Her eyes stung, but she had no more tears left to shed tonight. She swallowed past the lump in her throat. "Me too. I wasn't living with them anymore, but we were really close, and it was a huge blow. Suddenly I had lost not just my only family, but the two people I loved and depended on most in the world."

"I understand," he said, his voice low and sympathetic. "Just losing my own father was awful. I can't imagine losing both parents at the same time."

"I was devastated." She pressed her lips together, scratching the smooth fur of Bosco's ear. "But, like I told you, I was raised to be strong, and I knew my parents wouldn't want me to just succumb to grief and depression. So I kept on going, as best as I could."

He nodded, taking a swallow of his drink.

"I was living with my best friend, Brittney. We met our freshman year of college, and we stayed roommates through school. Then we moved into an apartment together in the city. She wanted to be an actress, but while she was working on that, she bartended at night." An unexpected wave of nostalgia washed over her, heavy and bittersweet. They'd had so much fun together, before everything happened. Seven years of wonderful memories, now tinged with deceit.

Clearing her throat, she continued. "I had the job at the brokerage firm, and I'd been dating a man who worked there for about a year when my parents had the accident. Nathan. He was a little older than me, and he was really there for me during the aftermath. He helped sort all the horrible details out so I could grieve. About six months later, when he proposed, I said yes."

His brows lifted. "You were engaged?"

She nodded. "For almost a year," she said, her voice breaking. "Sorry, this is hard for me."

"It's okay, Lark. Take your time."

She exhaled, leaning forward to pick up her glass from the table. Bosco's heavy weight shifted with her, but he stayed put, emitting a soft grunt of contentment when she settled again. "Anyway, I still lived with Brittney, but I often stayed at Nathan's apartment. It was nicer, and closer to my work. Then, a few weeks ago..." *Had it only been a few weeks?* It seemed like a lifetime ago now. "I got fired. It wasn't totally unexpected, since there was a merger and I knew some of the staff would get laid off. But the nature of the business means they keep these things very secret right up until they escort you out the door. They don't want any employees taking client contact info or sensitive materials.

"Still, I was really upset, and I hadn't even been given a moment to speak to Nathan before they made me leave. I kept calling him, but I got his voicemail. Like I said, his apartment was close, and Brittney slept days because of her late nights. So I went over to his place."

"Oh, no"

"Yeah. I let myself in, and I heard something, so I immediately went quiet. It was lunchtime on a Friday, so I'd fully expected the apartment to be empty. At first I was scared, but then I recognized the sounds. Nathan was having sex with someone, no question. Someone other than his fiancé." Her stomach clenched, filling with poison, and she knocked back a swig of whisky, nearly coughing at the harsh burn. "I almost turned and ran, but then I realized I had to catch him in the act. He had a way of talking his way out of things. So I stormed over and flung open the bedroom door."

"Was it...?"

"Brittney. Yes. My best friend and my fiancé, in bed together. It was...surreal, for lack of a better term. The image is seared into my brain. But I'm glad I saw it, because if I'd found out some other way, I never would have believed it."

He swore under his breath, shaking his head. Tendons rose along his arms in taut cords as his fists clenched. "What happened then?"

"There were gasps and curses and a few attempts to get me to 'just listen', but that's when I did run out the door. They were, you know, not dressed, so I outran them easily. I made it to my apartment to grab a few things, and Preston, and then I went to another friend's place. I haven't spoken one word to either of them since, and I blocked their numbers. So I don't even know how long it was going on for. Not that it matters. Even once is not something I'm going to get over, considering those two had become the people I loved and trusted the most in the world." She shrugged, attempting a wry smile. "Apparently I'm a great judge of character."

"No. Don't put this on yourself, even as a joke. You did nothing wrong."

"Well, I trusted the wrong people."

"They're the ones at fault here," he said firmly, his tone edged in steel. "What they did was horrible, and your former fiancé is lucky I don't know where he lives."

That brought a real grin to her face. "Believe me, I'd put my money on you in a fight. But it's done, and I'm really trying to move on. It's just…well, that kind of betrayal takes a toll."

"I get it. I'm sorry that happened, Lark."

"It's better that I found out before the wedding, I guess. Anyway, I'd gotten the news about inheriting this house right before that, so after about a week of crashing at my friend Madison's apartment, I decided to come here and regroup."

He locked eyes with her, holding her gaze. "I'm glad you came here." The simple words carried the weight of sincere emotions. Pausing, he scrubbed at his jaw. "Even though I know things haven't exactly been smooth going for you here, either."

Her chest tightened. After all this, he was still glad she had come into his life. "Well, bright side…you've renewed my faith in humanity. I'm grateful for everything you've done for me since I've been here, Jesse."

"I care about you. And I'm glad you felt comfortable enough to tell me what happened."

Another round of tears threatened, and she bent her head over the dog on her lap as she blinked them back. She sagged, the adrenaline that had been keeping her going suddenly draining from her system like water from a broken pipe. The few sips of whisky she'd taken swirled in its place, coursing sluggishly through her veins.

"Hey," he said softly, breaking the silence. "You must be wrecked. We should try to get some sleep." He stood up, crossing to her and extending his hand.

She nodded, readily accepting his help as she forced her wobbly legs to hold her upright. The stress of the past few hours was rapidly taking its toll. She retrieved her bag from the kitchen as he turned off the lights, then followed him up the stairs. With every step, a fresh wave of exhaustion seeped into her bones, turning her feet to lead. By the time they'd made it to the top, she was afraid she might collapse onto the dark wood of the hallway floor.

He paused by the open door to the master bedroom, gesturing farther down the hall. "There are two guest rooms, so you can choose whichever. Both should be made up."

The dogs filed into his room, and she watched as Bosco jumped onto the end of the bed. The sheets were thrown back on Jesse's side, presumably from his rush to respond to her screams. The windows stood open, letting in the cool breeze rolling in from the woods, and farther off, the Atlantic.

To her embarrassment, he picked up the longing on her face. "You can stay in here, with us, if you'd feel safer."

She was too tired to even pretend to demur. She gave him a grateful look. "I think I would." God, the mixed messages she'd been giving him this week. It was a wonder the man still spoke to her. "If you really don't mind," she added.

"I think I'll sleep better with you in here too."

Her heart fluttered, but she was pretty sure he wasn't referring to the possibility of sex. He just meant he'd be more likely to hear her if she had another sleepwalking incident. Of course, she'd snuck out of this bedroom before without waking him. But she wasn't about to bring that up.

She returned to his room after using the hall bathroom, her feet still slightly damp from a quick wash in the tub. He was already in bed, lying on his back and checking his phone. She padded around to the other side and climbed in slowly, as if not making sudden moves might make the situation less awkward.

"Move, Bosco," he instructed the dog. Bosco raised his head, a questioning look on his face, but he stayed put. Jesse huffed out a sigh, rolling his eyes. "Just push him out of the way."

"It's fine. He was here first." She had to bend her knees to fit into the available space, so she settled onto her side, facing Jesse.

He clicked off the light on the bedside table and the room slipped into darkness. "Night, Lark."

"Goodnight." His arm was close to her hand, and she reached down and touched her fingers to his as she drew in a breath. "I'm sorry I've built my walls so high," she said softly. "It's just...the wounds are still so fresh."

"I get it." He twined their fingers together, giving her hand a gentle squeeze. "You'll heal."

Deep inside her, something shifted, like a cramped muscle finally beginning to loosen. Clasping his hand, she closed her eyes as sleep reached up to claim her.

18

She stirred as he came back into the bedroom after his shower, and he stilled. He didn't want to wake her. But her eyelids fluttered open, a cloud of confusion creasing her brows before she remembered where she was. Pushing herself up against the headboard, she glanced over at him, a shy smile playing over her lips.

Christ, she was beautiful. Her expression was dreamy, her features slightly puffy from sleep and tears, and the combination revealed the vulnerable side of her she tried so hard to hide. Her tousled hair framed her face, and his rumpled T-shirt fell in soft folds over her breasts. "Hi," she murmured, tugging the covers up around her waist.

As they'd slept, their bodies had gravitated toward each other, and waking up with her spooned against him had been torture. He'd had to summon every ounce of willpower not to nuzzle her neck, kissing the tender skin along the curve up to her ear. Not to slip his hand under the cotton of her shirt—*his* shirt—and cup her breast. His palms remembered every rise and valley of her body, and it took superhuman control to keep his arm where it was, draped protectively over her waist, separated from her warm flesh by a layer of fabric. But he had no idea where they stood now. He wasn't sure where she wanted to go from here, and he wasn't sure where he wanted to go, either. Still, that knowledge wasn't enough to temper the desire ignited by the curl of her back against his chest, the press of her bottom into his hips. Exquisite, unrelenting agony.

"Hey," he replied, fighting to pull his thoughts away from the sight of her in his bed. And what they had done in that bed only six nights ago. "I was hoping I wouldn't wake you."

Her gaze ran over his bare torso, falling to the towel wrapped around his waist. Color rose in her cheeks, and she glanced away, toward the window. "It's fine. What time is it?"

He ignored the pulse of heat in his groin. "Almost seven. Listen, if you need more rest, you should just stay and go back to sleep."

"Oh, thanks, but I should probably get home. I have to work the lunch shift."

"Are you going to be okay, after so little sleep?"

She lifted a shoulder. "I should be. As long as I have coffee."

"That was my thinking too. There's plenty downstairs. Feel free to hang around and get your fill." He ran a hand through his damp hair, taking a moment to figure out the best way to approach the issue he'd been thinking about in the shower. "Listen, Lark...the woods thing has now happened twice, and there's no reason to believe it's going to stop until we figure everything out. You should consider staying here again tonight."

Her forehead creased. "I don't want to inconvenience you," she said, shaking her head.

"It's going to inconvenience me a hell of a lot more if I have to set up a tent by the river."

Surprise and amusement played across her face. "You wouldn't," she said with a giggle.

"Try me."

"But...I'm invading your space."

He took a step toward the bed, holding her gaze. "I don't mind waking up next to you. Although it was a definite test of my self-control." The last sentence tumbled out without permission, but hey, it was the truth. He may as well be honest.

"It was?" She caught her bottom lip in her teeth, her eyes darkening as her gaze lingered over his bare chest again. "I actually missed out on that part. The...uh...waking up next to you." She touched the bed beside her. "What time do you have to be at work?"

His body was already responding to the suggestive look on her face; the seductive tone of her voice fueled the fire. "I may be a little late this morning," he said, standing over her.

She reached out, tracing her finger across the ridge of abdominal muscles above his towel. "Maybe you had car trouble?"

He made a groaning noise of assent. "I noticed you're wearing my shirt."

His stomach quivered as her fingers continued their path. "I meant to return it to you. But I like wearing it. It reminds me of you," she added huskily.

"Consider it yours." He touched her breast beneath the fabric. "Right now, though, I'd prefer it on the floor."

She obediently raised her arms over her head, and he gathered the hem from her waist and slowly lifted it up, her hair spilling back out as he removed it and tossed it to the floor. "Better?" she asked.

"Much."

"Your turn." Her hands returned to the towel, and she tugged it until it puddled on the floor, joining his shirt.

DESPITE ONLY GETTING about four hours of sleep, she couldn't keep the smile off her face as she straightened her house before work. She actually caught herself dancing as she put the dishes away. She'd taken a shower and seen only her own face in the mirror—slightly pale, but familiar features made of flesh and blood. She'd fed Preston and played with him, and her good mood must have been contagious, because he'd jumped enthusiastically as she dangled a feathered toy from a wand above his head.

Now she had about an hour before she had to leave for work, and she had to devote some time to figuring out what to do about the car situation. She needed to get it back to its owner soon, and she'd done some trades at work to ensure she had both Saturday and Sunday off. Hopefully, Madison would let her crash one more night on the couch so she could break up the round-trip drive. But then there was the problem of *what* she was going to drive back. After she called Madison, she'd have to call some car rental places and find out what her options were.

She was still on the phone with Madison, wandering around the kitchen as they spoke, when she heard the bone-chilling noises coming from upstairs. Lark froze, gripping the phone as goosebumps prickled her skin. *Oh, God.* Wrenching sobs echoed through the room, drifting down through the ceiling.

"Lark?"

She jumped at the sound of Madison's voice coming through the line, her breath rushing out in an audible gasp. "What?" she yelped into the phone. Reining herself in, she quickly apologized, searching her brain for an excuse to end the conversation immediately. "Sorry, Madison…I…um, Preston's throwing up." She crept through the kitchen, toward the back staircase, as she added, "I have to run. Talk soon?" Her thumb hit the red end-call icon before the second syllable of Madison's "Okay" response made it through.

She paused on the landing, listening to the haunting sounds of grief and despair. The adrenaline flooding her veins told her to run away, the primal instinct blaring like an air raid siren. But she knew she had to force herself forward—avoidance would not help her solve this. Gripping the bannister, she climbed the stairs, her legs trembling, her heart thudding a wild staccato rhythm.

A fresh jolt of fear slammed into her as she peered down the hallway. The door to the front room stood open. She always, always kept it closed. Swallowing hard, she squared her shoulders. The ghost had already demonstrated it could manipulate things. The beckoning door was an unsettling sight, but it wasn't unprecedented. Pulling in a breath, she crept down the hall.

As she neared the room, the sobs slowed, broken by choked pauses. She could almost hear the strangled gasps for air, and her mind carried her back to her own emotional release at Jesse's last night. A thread of sympathy joined the dread and apprehension roiling through her as she forced herself to peek around the threshold.

Her eyes shot to the far bed automatically, searching for the seated figure she'd witnessed before. The filmy woman was there, but this time she was lying on her side, curled in a ball, her back facing Lark. Morning sunlight shone through the windows and into her transparent form, bleaching the already hazy lines of her phantom body. But slight movements in the shimmering air around her accompanied the soft weeping.

Lark gathered her courage. "Hello?" she croaked past the terror lodged in her throat.

The specter tore apart, like a wisp of clouds melting into the sky. The disembodied sounds lingered for a moment longer, finally disappearing, along with any potential clues.

Sagging against the doorway, she surveyed the room as she resumed breathing. Was that appearance supposed to tell her something? She felt compelled to take a closer look, despite the protests still raging from her internal alarm system. Dragging her feet forward, she crossed the room and stood over the far bed. Like before, the comforter revealed the faint outline of a recent presence. With a trembling hand, she reached down and touched the spot where Eva's face would have rested.

Cold. Damp. She snatched her hand away, reeling back as nausea churned in her stomach. So, so awful. Rubbing her fingers against her shorts, she slowly backed out of the room, keeping the bed in sight until she closed the door on it.

You're okay. Sucking in a shaky breath, she hurried down the hall and into the bathroom, avoiding her reflection as she washed the chill of ghostly tears off of her fingers. Reining in her spinning thoughts as she descended the stairs, she tried to focus. Could she conclude anything from this latest episode?

That front room had been Eva's. And at some point in her stay here, she had been very upset about something. Maybe Martha's death, and having to leave this house? Or missing her family, and her home in Poland?

Or was this apparition expressing something in the here and now, as opposed to the past? Things had happened that made it clear the ghost could react to things Lark did or said aloud. Was this grief and frustration over the fact that Lark was leaving for New York City?

She jotted the questions on a pad of paper, tapping the pen against her lips as she tried to put together theories in her head. What was Eva trying to tell her? What did her spirit need? She sighed, glancing over at the clock on the oven. Nearly time to leave for work.

Abandoning her notes, she poured yet another cup of coffee, heating it up before she trudged back upstairs to finish getting ready.

19

*T*he dogs raced ahead into the darkness, sensing Lark before Jesse caught sight of her. A thick layer of clouds had moved in this evening, obscuring the sky. Even the nearly full moon couldn't pierce the heavy blanket, and the woods were a collage of deep shadows and inky shapes.

They met on her side of the bridge, and he swept her into his arms, seizing her mouth in a lingering kiss. God, he was crazy about her. Even her scent was intoxicating—citrus and wildflowers. He nuzzled her neck as they parted, breathing her in.

"This feels clandestine," she whispered.

"I can live with that." He took her hand, leading them across the bridge. The dogs followed, their nails clicking on the weathered boards.

She laughed. "How was your day?"

"Pretty quiet, thankfully." It had been a long day, though, and he'd thought about her through most of it. He'd had a soccer game, so he'd stayed after hours at the clinic and grabbed a quick bite with the guys after. By the time he'd emerged from a shower and set out across his yard, the anticipation had become an electric current. "How was yours?"

"Um…work was fine. But I saw the ghost this morning." Her fingers tightened around his.

Alarm shot through his veins. "You okay?"

"Yes. I heard it—I mean, Eva, I guess—crying upstairs. In that front room, where I've seen her before. She was lying on one of the beds, sobbing, but when I spoke to her, she vanished."

He cleared his throat. "That's…unsettling."

"It was. But I'm trying to think of it in terms of clues. Like, is there something she's trying to communicate by showing me that? Right before it started, I was on the phone, talking to a friend about coming to New York."

A taut wire coiled in his chest. "What?"

"Sorry, I don't mean permanently. At least not right now. But I do need to get that car back to the owner, and since I switched some shifts around to have Saturday and Sunday off, I thought I'd go this weekend."

"How will you get back?"

"Well, I'm going to need some kind of transportation. I'm looking into a long-term rental, and I'll drive that back."

"Why don't I go with you? I can drive you back. Then you can rent a car here. It would be much cheaper."

"Hmm…that's true."

"I mean, unless you're in the market for a Jeep you can take four-wheeling on the beaches, you should be able to do better here, price-wise."

She chuckled. "Nope, I just need something that will get me to and from work, and maybe the store." She paused as they crested the hill. "But I don't want you to have to spend your weekend doing all that driving."

"I have off," he said with a shrug. "We can make a fun weekend out of it. You can show me around the city. I haven't been there since I was a kid," he added as he slid the back door open for her.

"That would be fun." She turned to meet his gaze in the bright lights of the kitchen. "But...I was going to stay on Madison's couch. She might notice if I have a guest."

He laughed, ushering the dogs in and closing the door against the swirl of tiny moths. "I think you've had enough of sleeping on couches. I'll find us a nice hotel."

She chewed on her lip. "Oh, I don't know. Anywhere decent is so expensive. Even for one night."

His gaze lingered on her mouth, and he lost the thread of the conversation for a moment. He shook his head to clear it. "It's fine. I make good money, Lark." When she wavered, he feigned exasperation, heaving an exaggerated sigh. "Also, I get a military discount. Does that make you feel better?"

The hint of a smile broke through the concern on her face. "Well, it *would* be fun..."

"Good. I'll even spring for two rooms, if you prefer privacy."

Her lips curved into a playful pout as she gave him a sultry look. "Oh, I don't know. I kind of enjoy our sleepovers."

His blood ran hot. "Yeah?" He raised his brows, taking a step closer to her. "As long as we're on the subject, I should let you know right now that you're still welcome to sleep in one of the guestrooms, if you want. And that if you don't, I'm going to have trouble keeping my hands off you."

Peering up at him, she ran her palms over his forearms and along his biceps. "We seem to be on the same page." Her hands slid down his chest, slipping under the bottom of his shirt. "So, no guestroom."

He caught the sides of her face, lowering his mouth to hers. Heat turned to flames as he deepened the kiss, his body demanding more. *Lark.* Need built like a violent storm, fierce and unrelenting.

Her hands continued their downward path, stroking the length of his erection through the fabric of his shorts. A groan rumbled in his throat. His stomach muscles quivered as her fingers dipped beneath the elastic waistband.

Her kisses trailed along his neck, her teeth grazing his skin. She sank to her knees, and a ragged breath tore from his chest.

"If you don't stop, we're not going to make it beyond *this* room."

She didn't stop. His fingers plunged into her hair as she took him in her mouth.

Christ, she was killing him. His muscles tightened as sensations rocked through him. Every nerve ending in his body crackled, every second brought him closer to the edge. But he was desperate to ravish her first. "I need to be inside you," he said, his voice rough with urgency.

They made it upstairs, trailing discarded clothes along the

way. Collapsing on the bed in a tangle of limbs, he rolled on top of her, pinning her arms over her head. His mouth closed over her nipple as she squirmed and moaned beneath him.

"Jesse," she gasped, bucking her hips.

His lips tugged at the sensitive flesh as he held her captive. She strained against him, her head thrown back, exposing the delicate column of her throat. Releasing her wrists, he kissed his way down the taut skin of her belly. Tiny tremors quaked beneath his touch. He nuzzled the inside of her thighs, savoring her pleading moans. She cried out when his mouth moved between her legs, her fists clutching at the comforter. *God, the taste of her...he would never get enough.*

Her muscles tightened around him as he teased her with his tongue, and his own need built to an undeniable force, snapping his last thread of control. He levered himself over her, locking eyes with her in the shadows, their jagged breaths mingling for an agonizing moment of anticipation. She clung to him, arching her back, attempting to close the distance between their bodies. "Please," she rasped, her voice thick with desire.

He drove himself into her, and she gasped, digging her fingernails into his back. He stilled, allowing her to set the rhythm, then matched it with powerful strokes. His body sought to claim hers with each deep thrust, joining them together. Violent spasms rocked her hips as she climaxed, and she clutched at his shoulders, shuddering. Her tiny whimpers and moans filled his ears, and he let go, exploding inside her with a fierce jolt of pleasure. Her legs shook as another wave of sensations ripped through her, the faint sting of her nails dragging down his back flaring, then easing. When her hands slid weakly along his slick skin, he collapsed onto her, reveling in the feel of her beneath him, the shared beat of their thundering hearts. She drew in a trembling breath, and he shifted his weight to avoid crushing her.

"You okay?" he murmured playfully as he gathered her into his arms.

"Well, if someone asked me my name right now, I'm not sure I could remember," she joked, curling into him with a contented sigh. "Other than that, I'm beyond okay. Like, a million miles north of okay."

"Me, too," he agreed with a chuckle, kissing the top of her head as she laid her cheek on his chest. Her hair spilled over his shoulders like a soft curtain, and she splayed her hand across his abdomen. "We're pretty good at that."

She made a satisfied sound of agreement. As her breathing slowed, she added, "Can we just stay here for a while?"

He tugged at the comforter, pulling the fabric toward him until he found the side edge. Settling it over their joined bodies, he brushed his fingers along her temple. "We can stay here all night."

THE HIGHWAY UNSPOOLED in front of Jesse's truck as they made their way back toward the Cape on Sunday evening. She smiled as he sang along to a song on his playlist. He had an amazing voice, deep and melodic. She couldn't carry a tune to save her life.

Closing her eyes, she savored the peacefulness of the truck's cab. When they'd arrived in New York City, the throngs of people and the snarled traffic had felt like an assault to her senses, now that she was used to the clean air and open spaces of Truro. She was shocked to find herself slightly over-whelmed by the noises, smells, and crowds swirling through every block. The bustle and energy were still exciting, but somehow, it felt different. More like a destination, and less like home.

Although the trip had been short, they'd had a good time in Manhattan. After returning the borrowed car, they'd checked into a hotel in Times Square before noon on Saturday. Despite the muggy heat, they'd rented bikes and pedaled all around Central Park. Tired and sweaty, they'd returned to the hotel to clean up, and now her cheeks warmed as she thought of the intimate shower they'd taken together. She'd brought him to some of her favorite spots for happy hour and dinner, and they'd ended up at a piano bar at the end of the night. This morning, they'd awoken early to fit in a few touristy activities before meeting Madison for a late lunch.

She'd loved sharing it all with Jesse. But there was one distressing thing she hadn't shared with him, and it continued to plague her thoughts as she pretended to doze.

She'd awoken in the hotel room in the middle of the night —shortly after 1:00 in the morning, actually—standing by the door, pulling on the knob. Thankfully, the safety lever across the top had prevented her from actually getting out into the hallway—not only did she have no idea what she might have done, but she'd also been completely naked. She'd lingered there as awareness dawned, blinking in confusion, with her heart racing and her mind clutching to the shreds of a vivid dream.

A nightmare, really. It had transported her to her house in Truro, and she'd been frantically trying to get out the front door. Something terrible had happened, or was about to happen, or maybe both. Screams lodged in her throat as her clammy hands twisted the knob, and the same panicked thought blared repeatedly through her mind: *she had to get out, she had to find help.*

But it hadn't been *her* mind, exactly. Lark was certain these were Eva's memories. One long-ago night, Eva had run through the woods seeking assistance, and Lark's sleepwalking incidents were echoing the past. And when Lark found herself struggling to escape the hotel room, a terrifying realization set in—Eva could reach her *here*, in New York City. Reaching her less than a mile away from the Cape house, in Jesse's bedroom, would not be impossible. She wasn't safe anywhere.

Should she tell him? None of this was solid, factual information. She was just guessing, based on that uncomfortable feeling of not being alone in her head when she emerged from the dream. But if she mentioned her theory, Jesse was going to worry even more than he already was. What more could he do besides sleep next to her every night? She wasn't going to ask him to stay up and sit over her while she slept. Could they barricade her in? Handcuff her to the bed? Despite her current agitation, a wicked smile tugged at her lips at this internal suggestion. He might be up for that, but with very different intentions. Restraints designed to keep her from running out into the night in the throes of a nightmare were a lot less tantalizing.

This was definitely more than he'd signed up for. He should not have to be her babysitter. Besides, last night's dream could have just been her own memory of the dreams she'd had at her house. It was all just so convoluted.

Turning back toward him, she admired his handsome profile as he stared out the windshield. Sensing her gaze, he glanced over and smiled, reaching for her hand. "Good nap, beautiful?"

She made an 'umm' noise to avoid an outright lie. Twining her fingers through his, she pushed last night's incident out of her mind.

20

*I*t was time. John had to know the truth. She'd spent the last few months in a haze of worry and doubt, with hope and fear warring on a daily basis. But Eva was sure now—she was pregnant.

Of course, he'd be shocked at first...although if she understood the biology correctly, this was not an unforeseeable development. As an older—married—man, he must have known the risks. But he loved her, and he'd been insistent, pushing her to show her love for him. Coming to her room in the middle of the night with increased frequency and urgency over the last six months. After the initial surprise, eventually he would accept it, and he would be pleased.

If he came to her tonight, she would tell him. She left her room, padding down the hallway to use the bathroom. Patting her face dry, she stared at her reflection in the mirror over the sink. The morning sickness had carved her features into sharper angles, but the nausea was passing now, and she was starting to gain weight. There was no sign of the glow her mother had spoken of as a sign of pregnancy, but Eva still felt it inside…a new life. A new chance at having a family, after all she'd lost.

As she came out, she heard the door to the master bedroom open, and her heart fluttered as she turned to face John. He closed the door softly, then approached her, settling his hand on her back as he steered her back toward her own room.

Before he could guide her toward the bed, she slowed, turning to face him. Taking his hand, she pulled in a deep breath. "John, I have news. I…we're having a child." Flames licked her cheeks, and she dropped her gaze as she pressed his hand to her belly. Her heart pounded as his palm rested on the slight swell protruding beneath her nightgown.

His eyes widened. "What? That can't be. I've been…careful."

The fiery warmth burning her face spread to a searing heat radiating to every inch of her skin. He always tried to spill his seed outside of her body. But somehow, a baby had taken hold. She had vacillated between labeling it a miracle from God, or a punishment from Him. These past few weeks, though, had brought several Sunday sermons from John that made her understand this was indeed a gift, for both of them. After all, they loved each other.

In truth, she wasn't smart enough to figure out what would come next, how they would proceed. But John was. He had God's ear. He had dedicated his life to serving the Lord, and God wouldn't send them this blessing unless it was meant to be.

He snatched his hand away from her body, out of her grasp,

as though she harbored some contagious disease. "This is a mistake," he insisted, his voice low and firm.

She shook her head, confused. "No. I haven't had my courses in months. I've been ill in the mornings. I'm certain."

He backed away, out into the hallway. "No, I mean this is a mistake." He gestured between the two of them. "You were sent to tempt me, and I was weak."

Dread coiled through her. *What?* No…John had brought her here to help with Martha. And then he had pursued her—relentlessly—pledging his love to her, promising to marry her someday, when he was free.

She blinked, trying to understand. "But…I thought you wanted to be with me…after Martha…" Her words faded away, the sentence too awful to complete out loud. She swallowed back a sob. "That's what you told me."

"Lower your voice," he hissed, glancing over his shoulder toward the closed door of the master bedroom. He grabbed her upper arm. "Obviously you've misunderstood something. And you've gotten yourself into trouble. You'll have to leave."

What was happening? She gaped at him, barely registering the pain of his fingers digging into her soft flesh. *She'd* gotten herself into trouble? He wasn't going to take any responsibility? And now he was telling her she had to leave? Fear and confusion twisted in her belly. This wasn't right. "But…I can't leave. I have nowhere to go." Her voice broke, and she dropped her head into her hands.

"An unwed mother's home."

Panic exploded in her chest, sharp and savage. "What?" she

gasped, snapping her gaze back to his. "No! I've heard the stories of those places. They'll take my baby. I won't go."

"Quiet down!" he hissed, lowering his face over hers. Something dangerous glinted in the depths of his eyes. "You will. You can't stay here."

The hallway tilted as her vision swam. Her world was crashing down around her, again. The unfairness of it all made her want to scream. But Martha was asleep in the bedroom behind them. "You said you loved me," she whispered past the lump in her throat.

He dragged his fingers through his hair, his head lowering in a small gesture of shame. "You cannot stay here. Martha will know."

A surge of hope bloomed. "I'll say the baby is someone else's."

He shook his head. "She already has suspicions about us. People in town have been gossiping. My standing is at stake. My livelihood is at stake. I'm the moral leader of this community."

She wrapped her arms around her chest in an attempt to quell the shaking. How could he betray her like this, after all the promises he'd made? "I won't go," she insisted, the tremor in her voice undermining her words.

His gaze darted about the hallway before fixing back on her face. Cords bulged from his neck like taut ropes. "Then you will get rid of it," he said through gritted teeth.

She sucked in a breath. "What? No!"

"Hush!"

Her legs threatened to buckle, but she forced herself to stay upright. "I will not kill our baby! It's against the law. It's dangerous." She narrowed her eyes at him to deliver her final argument. "It's a sin."

The knob to the master bedroom turned, and both their heads swiveled as the door swung open. Martha stood in the threshold, confusion clouding her gaunt face. "What's going on?" Her sleepy gaze sharpened as it flicked between them. "John? Eva? What's wrong?"

Martha! Martha would be her savior. Clutching her stomach, she moved away from John. "I've fallen pregnant," she blurted out.

A heavy silence hung in the air as they all traded shocked glances. Martha reeled backwards, reaching out to grip the doorway. She brought her free hand to her mouth as she regarded them both, understanding dawning in her eyes. "You…are expecting a baby?"

This was it—her way out. Martha desperately wanted a baby, even though the likelihood of that happening had diminished along with her health. "Yes," Eva confirmed with a rushed breath of relief. "I'm expecting a baby." John reached out to silence her, but she darted away. "I'm pregnant with John's baby, and he wants to kill it."

Martha's eyes were glinting daggers as she turned them on her husband. "What? John? Is this true?"

Dark red rage colored his face as he swung his gaze between them. "Martha, this does not concern you. Go back to bed."

Martha's thin lips pressed into a tight line. Stepping

forward, she shouldered her way past Eva. "I think it does. Is this young woman pregnant with your child?"

John glared at her, refusing to respond. Eva took her chance. Latching on to Martha's arm, she pleaded for help. "Please, Mrs. Holloway! I have nowhere else to go. I have no family left. This baby is all I have...I cannot kill it."

Martha pulled Eva behind her own slight frame. "You have dishonored our marriage, John. You have committed a grievous sin. But a miracle has arisen from your sin. We will be blessed with a baby, after all these years. We will raise this child as our own."

John's hands balled into fists. "We will not! Everyone knows you are barren. Everyone will see that Eva's with child. I will not lose my standing in our community over this." He stabbed a finger over Martha's shoulder at Eva. "She is a temptress! She led me astray, but I will not let her ruin me."

Martha stiffened. "You will not deprive me of this child. It is a gift from God."

"And you will not defy me," he retorted, spittle flying from his lips. "'Wives, submit to your own husbands, as to the Lord. For the husband is the head of the wife, even as Christ is the head of the church.'"

"'Do not kill the innocent and righteous, for I will not acquit the wicked,'" Martha shot back, answering his Biblical quote with her own.

"I am the man of this house. She will not have this baby. She is a whore sent by the devil, and I will kill her before I let her bring shame on this family!" He lunged forward, arms reaching for Eva.

"No!" Martha shouted, stepping into his path. "I won't let you hurt her!"

John's hands missed Eva, latching instead onto his wife's frail shoulders. As Eva backed away, the couple struggled, their cries echoing through the hallway. Years of anger and frustration played out in a moment that seemed to stretch each second into an eternity. Then suddenly time sped up as John's final shout was accompanied by a powerful shove that sent Martha reeling.

Eva froze as Martha's body bounced off the bannister railing and spun toward the stairs.

———

LARK FOUGHT to surface from the horrific dream, struggling against the layers of sleep weighing her down. In one brief moment of consciousness, she understood that she'd just witnessed Martha's death through Eva's eyes. But the power holding her captive was too strong. Too determined. She was aware of her bare feet sliding to the floor of Jesse's bedroom as the need to flee built deep within her, drowning everything else out.

Then nothing beyond the ominous thudding of Martha's body tumbling down the stairs. Cracking bones and a wheezing moan. The sickening fear of being next.

Run! Hurry! She needed to save herself. Save the baby.

hey both stared at Martha's motionless body for an agonizing moment as time stood still. Was she alive? Eva willed her legs to move, to take advantage of this horrible turn of events. Martha couldn't help her now. She had to get away from John, before he carried out his threats.

She broke their stunned spell, darting from the corner of the hallway where she'd been cowering and racing down the stairs. She focused on the front door to keep her gaze away from Martha's crumpled body. His footsteps pounded behind her, but he crouched over Martha as she flung open the door. The darkness beckoned, cool autumn air embracing her. And then his command followed her out: "Stop!"

Stumbling down the porch steps, she slowed, her head swiveling. Where could she go? She could never outrun him. She needed to get to the woods, where she could hide. Closer to the house on the other side of the river, where maybe someone would hear her cries for help.

Decision made, she tore around the side of the house and down the sloping hill of the yard, her breath hitching in jagged gasps. Was Martha dead? Was she next? She had to save the baby!

The full moon hung above the trees, its reddish hue illuminating her flight. But the bright moonlight would make it more difficult to hide. She could hear John behind her now, gaining distance on her, but she refused to allow herself to look back. She couldn't afford to lose her momentum. Or to trip and fall. Instead of angling toward the path, she plunged into the woods as soon as she approached the tree line.

"Help!"

Brambles reached up to rip her flesh; low branches slapped at her face. The pain barely registered beyond the panic. "Help me!" But it was too late. His heaving breaths filled her ears as he closed the distance between them.

SOMETHING cold and wet nudged his cheek, and Jesse rolled over. An insistent paw scraped his chest, and the accompanying whine finally dragged him from a deep slumber. With a sigh, he blinked in the darkness, wrinkling his nose as Bosco panted into his face. The pit bull stood over him on the bed, and Benny turned in nervous circles on the floor, his nails clicking against the wood. What was going on?

He stretched his arm out, searching for Lark. His hand found only empty sheets, cool to the touch. "Lark?" he said, suddenly wide awake. Bosco let out a sharp bark, scrambling to the floor.

Where was she? Sitting up, he snapped on the bedside lamp and scanned the room. Empty, and the door to the master bath was open, the light off. "Lark?" he called again, his voice rising with concern. He tossed back the covers and climbed out of bed, pulling on the shorts that had landed on the floor when they'd torn each other's clothes off earlier.

His pulse accelerated as he strode to the door and called out again, even louder. Had she gone down to the kitchen to get something to eat? His mind flashed to the note he'd found weeks ago, and he scrubbed his jaw. She wouldn't have left like that, would she? They'd moved beyond that. Plus, they'd agreed it was safer for her to sleep here, after the second late-night scare in the woods.

The woods. Could she have fallen into that same nightmarish trance *here*? Dread clutched at him as his gaze fell on the two agitated dogs. But he'd always heard her cries for help before, even when she'd been on the other side of the river. His eyes shot to the window and his blood turned icy. He'd shut the bedroom windows against the evening's sticky heat, turning on the air conditioner to cool the house. With the windows closed, in his heavy sleep, he may not have heard her pleas for help. But the dogs had.

He rushed to the top of the stairs, the dogs at his heels. The front door stood open.

JOHN CAUGHT the back of her nightgown, and she stumbled, arms flailing for balance. "My wife is dead!" he growled as they continued their forward momentum together, locked in a horrific dance. "Devil!"

No, she tried to cry, but she couldn't catch her breath. Fear sliced through her as he gripped her waist, pushing her toward the bank of the river. *No no no.* He shoved her down, falling with her as she landed on her knees. "Please, no," she whimpered between hitching sobs. How was this happening? He knocked her forward, using the weight of his own body to pin her to the ground. "'You must purge the evil from among you,'" he muttered, his voice trancelike.

The river caught the ends of her hair as he forced her head toward the water. Images of her family shuffled through her mind, and she prayed to them for help. *Please, Mama. Tata. Babcia. Help me. Help my baby.*

His strong hands pushed her face under, and panic seized her, driving out every thought beyond the primal will to survive. Thrashing her arms, she struggled for purchase, but her hands only connected with the cold water, slapping weakly at the surface. Bubbles trailed from her nose as she fought for her life, the last of her air rushing out into the current.

SHE WAS DYING. It was Eva's memory, but it was Lark's body. Lark's face, pinned beneath the water. Lark's lungs, screaming for air. Lark's brain, begging for oxygen. Lark was going to die experiencing the final moments of Eva's tragic life.

No! The word flashed through her mind as she splashed at the surface of the river with numb hands. She was being held down, drowned, by something too strong to fight against. *I understand, Eva,* she begged silently. *John killed Martha, and he killed you and your baby. I understand now! I know what happened!*

Blood pounded in her ears, the pressure building with every painful thud. A barbed-wire vise tightened inside her chest, ripping at her flailing heart. Every cell in her body demanded she take a breath. Now.

Pain bulged behind her eyes, filling her skull as consciousness seeped away. With the last ounce of her strength, she struggled to lift her head against the force holding her captive. But it was impossible. She couldn't move. She was trapped in a nightmare from the past. *What do you want, Eva? I understand now! Please!*

Her hair swirled through the current, tangling in her fingers as they went limp. *Air. Need air.* The instinct to take a breath was too much to resist. Succumbing, she sucked the river into her lungs, and blackness descended.

22

The brutal pain was gone, the fire in her lungs vanquished. But a hazy sense of confusion remained. Where was she? Lost. Floating. Untethered.

Far off in the distance, a light beckoned. A gentle force seemed to be tugging her toward it, but a horrifying scene held her in place. The woods were now below her, the moonlight rippling on the dark river like tiny flames. And her body lay sprawled beside the bank, pale and lifeless.

A sound registered. A steady snick of metal hitting dirt. Grunts of effort, the clang of a blade against rock. Her field of vision expanded, as though she were being lifted skyward by a balloon.

At the edge of the woods, where the trees gave way to the backyard of the house she'd called home for the last year, John was digging. A large tangle of wild bushes had been unearthed and set aside. Through the darkness, she watched the hole grow deeper and wider.

Then she watched as he dragged her body through the woods and rolled it into the gaping earth. He replaced the dirt, replanting the bushes and scattering pine needles. Over what had just become her grave. And her child's.

Carrying the shovel, John trudged back up to the house. Eva could no longer see the distant light, or feel its warmth. All she felt was grief and rage, so she followed the man who had caused it all.

HE RACED TOWARD THE WOODS, his heart pounding, the dogs galloping beside him. He hadn't bothered to try to keep them inside as he'd shot out the open front door. They didn't wander or play, apparently sensing the dire urgency of the late night run.

Please don't let me be too late. Please. Please. He repeated the silent prayer in his head as he pushed his legs harder. With a surge of speed, he brought the river into view. Oh, God. She was there, hanging limply over the bank, in exactly the same spot he'd found her before. Instead of bothering with the bridge, he tore right into the river, splashing through the hip-deep water to get to her. "Lark!"

She didn't respond. Her naked body was still and lifeless in the moonlight, her arms dangling in the water. Please, no.

He hoisted her upper body out of the water the second he reached her, and horror surged through him as her head lolled forward, heavy with water, devoid of life. "Please, Lark," he begged her as he dragged her up the river bank. "Wake up."

But she wasn't asleep, caught in a dream like the other times. No breath lifted her chest or warmed his cheek, and his trembling fingers found no pulse. She was dead.

"No!" he yelled, rolling her onto her side. Water trickled from her mouth and nose. He flipped her onto her back again and titled her head, pinching her nose and covering her lips with his. He pushed two full breaths into her lungs, the immediately locked his hands over her breastbone and began chest compressions. "Come on, Lark," he murmured as he counted. "Come on, baby."

He administered another set of rescue breaths, forcing oxygen into her lungs. As he lifted his head to resume compressions, a torrent of water gushed from her mouth. A gurgling noise rattled her throat, and she expelled more water in a violent fit of coughing.

Relief crashed over him, and all he wanted to do was yank her up into his arms in a grateful embrace. But his military and medical training kept him focused. He rolled her to her side again, allowing the river water to drain from her lungs. As she retched, he did his best to assess her vital signs, pressing his fingers into the inside of her cold wrist. Her pulse was weak, but it was there. Thank you, God.

He wished he had his phone. And a blanket. He rubbed his hands over her body, trying to warm her flesh. When her coughing stopped and her breathing steadied, she turned her face up to look at him. "I—" she croaked, sputtering again.

"Shh. Don't try to talk. You're going to be fine, okay? Just rest and focus on breathing."

She nodded, but as he lifted her into his arms, she tried again. "Drowned," she managed.

"But you're okay now."

"No. Eva drowned. I know what happened now." A shuddering cough wracked her body. "I saw it all."

"We'll talk about it later, okay? Right now you need to save your strength. We're going back to the house, and then we're going to the hospital."

She made a low sound of disapproval, but this was not an argument she would win. Explaining exactly what had happened to the paramedics might be difficult, but he was calling an ambulance the second they got back to the house. He'd have to bend the truth, leaving out the details involving the supernatural. Thoughts swirled through his brain, but he pushed them away. The only thing that mattered was making sure she was completely out of danger. He shifted her weight, finding his balance, and carried her out of the woods, the dogs trailing behind them like silent sentries.

23

*S*he dragged her eyes open as murmuring voices penetrated her sleep. Jesse was sitting beside her, speaking softly to the nurse placing a new flower arrangement on the ledge by the window. He squeezed her hand gently as he noticed her waking up.

"Hey," she said groggily, clearing her throat. She glanced at the window, trying to judge the time. Weak sunlight filtered into the hospital room, and she guessed it was evening now. She'd been in and out of sleep all afternoon.

He thanked the departing nurse as he poured water from the pitcher resting on the swiveling table. "Hey, beautiful," he replied, handing Lark the plastic cup.

She rolled her eyes, accepting the water. "I'm sure." Glancing back toward the window, she admired the new flower arrangement. She'd already received several—one from Jesse's vet clinic, care of Diane, one from The Boatyard, and a small plant from some of the co-workers she was closest to. It was more than she expected, since she'd only been here a little over a month and hadn't exactly gone out of her way to make friends. People here were kind. A pang of gratitude swelled in her chest.

He followed her gaze. "Those are from my mom, and her crack investigative team at the community. They have some ideas about what really happened, but Mom said they'd keep it to themselves."

She smiled over the rim of the cup. "That's so nice of them. Please tell them thank you for me until I can do it myself." Running her hand through her hair, she grimaced at the smell of the river still lingering in the snarled strands. "So…I'm assuming the entire town knows at this point. How's the gossip?"

The corners of his lips twitched into a grin as he lifted a shoulder. "Well, the news that we've been shacking up is certainly out."

She flushed, but it had been unavoidable. In the end, the story they'd told stayed close to the truth. Lark claimed she'd taken a sleeping pill occasionally associated with sleepwalking, and she'd ended up wandering out of Jesse's house, where they'd been staying together. The dogs had woken him, and he'd found her unconscious in the river. He'd been able to resuscitate her, so she likely hadn't been submerged very long. As to how she ended up in the river, they speculated she fell in, maybe hit her head. Of course, the doctors could find no bumps or bruises to corroborate that, but since Lark maintained she'd been asleep the whole time and had no memory of anything beyond waking up to Jesse performing CPR, there wasn't much else to go on.

Lark *did* have a memory of it, though. Or at least Eva's memories of what had happened that awful night. As Jesse was helping her get dressed while they waited for the ambulance, she gave him a hurried version of what she'd seen. Since then, they'd discussed it in more detail during the few stretches of time they'd been alone throughout her hospital stay. So far, her tests showed no permanent damage, but the doctors insisted on holding her a full 24 hours to make sure no adverse effects developed. That meant she'd be here until early tomorrow morning.

She certainly hadn't expected Jesse to stay with her all day. But he'd had Diane cancel all his appointments for today and tomorrow. In fact, he hadn't left her side, unless forced to when she was undergoing tests. Her heart did a little flip as he winked at her.

"Sorry about that," she said, scrunching up one side of her mouth. "I hope you don't mind."

Confusion flickered over his features. "What? People knowing we're together? Of course not."

She couldn't keep the sappy grin off her face. *Together.* A thrill of happiness warmed her blood. This amazing man, who'd saved her life, saved Preston's life, dropped everything to stay with her at the hospital, and had pretty much been her savior since she'd arrived, had just said they were together. And that he was fine with everyone knowing.

Being with him was what she wanted, too. Despite the past betrayals that had wounded her so deeply, despite the vow she'd made to never give her heart away again, she wanted a relationship with him. She supposed a near-death experience had a way of making a person reexamine their choices.

"Are *you* okay with it?"

She nodded her head vigorously, sending a twinge of pain from last night's struggles through her neck. "I am," she said, reaching back with her free hand to rub the sore muscles. "I want us to be...together. And I want everyone to know."

He twined their fingers together, brushing the pad of his thumb over her skin. "It's official, then." Leaning forward, he kissed her gently. Lowering his voice, he added, "Even if learning what happened to Eva stops the haunting, I'm hoping you'll still spend the nights with me."

She lifted her eyebrows, feigning suspicion of his motives.

"Not just because of that," he said, laughing. "You know I like having you around all the time. But I also want to keep you safe."

She squeezed his fingers. "You do a good job of it," she said, her voice thick with emotion. Swallowing past the lump in her throat, she whispered, "What *are* we going to do about Eva?"

He glanced toward the open door. "Hang on." Releasing her hand, he got up from his chair and shut the door to her room. "So, I did some research on our options while you were asleep." He raked his fingers through his hair as he sat back down. "Do you need more water?" he asked, gesturing toward her drained cup.

"No, thanks." She chewed on her lip, waiting to hear what Jesse had found out.

"First of all, I'm going to search for her remains myself, once we're home and you can show me where to dig."

A tiny wave of nausea swirled through her stomach, but she nodded. "Okay. We may as well confirm she's there before we start anything."

"Right. Assuming we find bones, there are fairly clear procedures we're supposed to follow. We notify the police, they come out and make sure it appears we've dug up human bones, as opposed to animal bones. If they believe that's the case, they'll call in the medical examiner."

"Then what?"

"Well, things get murky after that. First we're going to have to explain how we found the bones. Assuming you don't want to mention the ghost and the visions, I was thinking we say we were doing some yardwork down there, clearing some brush or something, and the dogs kept digging in that spot."

"It's feasible, I guess. Although what we'd be doing clearing brush at the edge of the woods might raise a few questions."

He sighed. "Exactly. And then, we're going to have to explain why we think we know who it is. My mom and her friends can help with that, since they knew about Eva. And you can say you found her name mentioned in the family Bible."

"That works."

"Obviously, they're not going to just take our word for it. They'll want to take the bones and test them. At the very least, they'll be able to determine that the bones are around 70 years old at this point, which should rule out hanging on to them as part of a cold case. But I don't see how they'd be able to positively identify her, given that we don't even know her last name, and it's doubtful she has any close relatives, since she lost everyone in the war."

This *was* a difficult situation. She made an hmm sound as she waited for him to continue.

"At that point, it becomes completely unclear who becomes responsible for her remains. What we *don't* want is for her to end up in a box in a basement somewhere. So we'll just have to work really hard to get her properly buried. We'll have to deal with the town leaders, but I'm on several boards, and I know them all personally. I think I can make things move quickly. As quickly as a town government can, anyway. Then we would have to find a cemetery that will take her."

Her stomach clenched as the graveyard surrounding the local church flashed through her mind. "Not where *he's* buried."

"No. We'll find a different one. We can get a headstone that at least lists her first name, and have a small service."

"I can't ask you to pay for all of that. A cemetery plot probably costs a lot, not to mention a headstone."

He waved her objection away. "I have the money. I'm not worried about that. Besides, you're not asking, I'm offering." He picked up her hand again, enclosing it between both of his. "I'm just glad you're okay, Lark. And I'm hoping we can make this right for Eva, so please don't worry about the cost."

She frowned, but she knew he was right. What was important was righting the wrong committed decades ago. By someone in *her* family. Her stomach lurched again. At least

John had been a very, very distant relative. "You said we had options, right? Like, plural?"

"Well, sort of. The other option is we don't tell anyone. We move her ourselves, mark the gravesite ourselves, and put her to rest somewhere away from the property where she was murdered."

She sucked in a breath. "Is that...legal?"

A grim expression crossed his face as he tilted his head. "Well, yes and no. There aren't federal or state laws covering who exactly is in charge of unclaimed bodies. In Massachusetts, it's not illegal to bury a person on private property, so if we decide to move her from our property, we could try to find a place on private land somewhere else. With the owner's permission, of course, so there's that problem. But this is Cape Cod...there are all sorts of old family plots around, so it's not an impossible scenario. Technically, though, you're supposed to get the town's permission before you do something like that, so that could raise some flags."

She shook her head. "I don't think that's a good idea. It might be an easier path, but it could be bad for your career. Or your military status. You said before that there are pretty clear procedures to follow if a person finds bones. I know we'll face a lot of questions, but I think that's what we have to do. Find the bones, then call the police."

A beat of silence stretched out, broken only by a faint scratching sound as he scrubbed his palm over his jaw. "It's not just that it will be difficult, with all the questions and the red tape. It will throw us right back into the spotlight, too. I'll do my best to keep things as quiet as possible at first, but this is going to be big news for a while. Are you prepared for that?"

"I can handle it if you can." Inhaling, she held his gaze. "Together?"

He nodded. "Together."

24

*T*wo weeks after the bones had been found, Lark was sure Eva was gone. While she spent the nights with Jesse, she spent most of her days here, and there had been no more frightening occurrences. No sign of anything paranormal. And perhaps the best indication was Preston. He swaggered around the house with no hesitation at all. If she napped in the master bedroom, he was right there with her. She'd even wandered into the front guest room a few times, just to be sure, and Preston had casually followed her, showing curiosity but no fear.

She glanced out the front window as she dumped her laundry onto the couch to fold it. The media hype had died down at this point, thankfully. There'd been a few vans and reporters with cameramen taking images of the house after the initial discovery. The excavation took a little longer than they'd expected, due to an investigation to determine whether Jesse had unearthed a Native American burial site during his staged yardwork project. No one in authority was willing to take their guess that it was in fact the remains of a Polish immigrant from the post-WWII time period as fact. But now, it seemed like things were moving in the right direction. The wheels were turning slowly, but they were turning.

She often thought about that night, and what she'd seen through Eva's eyes. Her heart ached for the poor, terrified young woman, and the unborn child. Lark hoped that Eva had somehow found her way back to that distant light they'd glimpsed together, now that her remains had been discovered, and the circumstances of her death revealed.

There was, of course, a great deal of gossip flying around town as to what those circumstances were. Given that the body had been found in an unmarked grave, and a disappearance never reported, most everyone had come to the conclusion that John had done something awful to the young woman living in his house. While nothing could be done to hold him accountable now, at least the truth was finally out.

She stacked the folded clothes, setting aside her bathing suit and a towel. She was meeting some of the girls from work at the beach today. It wasn't a huge deal, but at the same time, it felt significant. It hadn't just been Nathan who scarred her—it had been Brittney too. Forming new friendships, however casual at this point, was progress, even though it made her feel vulnerable.

She stuffed the towel into a big canvas bag by the door, pulling her phone out to check if there were any changes to the plan. In the group text, there was just chatter about what snacks people were bringing and who had extra sunscreen, but she had a message from Jesse as well: "Have fun today, can't wait to see you tonight."

She pressed the phone screen against her chest, closing her eyes as a wave of joy coursed through her. The way she felt about Jesse made her wonder if she'd even really been in love with Nathan.

Her insides tightened as the word 'love' replayed in her mind. Did this mean what she felt for Jesse was love? Even after only knowing each other for six weeks?

They'd been through a lot together already, and she knew him well enough to know what kind of person he was. If she wasn't already in love, she knew she was falling fast. And while it was scary, it was also wonderful and exhilarating. Smiling to herself, she texted him back.

25

The smell of bacon pulled him from sleep, and he blinked groggily as he reached for Lark. Her side of the bed was empty, but he had a feeling these two things were linked together. Pushing himself up to sitting, he glanced around the room. The dogs weren't there, and he had a feeling their absence was also linked to the alluring aroma. He climbed out of bed, his stomach growling in anticipation as he threw on clothes.

He found her in the kitchen, standing in front of the stovetop with her back to him. Her fiery hair was pulled up into a messy knot, and she was wearing a dark blue T-shirt—one of his—and a pair of tiny plaid pajama shorts. She looked adorable. And slightly frazzled, as she transferred bacon onto a napkin-lined plate while simultaneously trying to flip pancakes. The dogs gave him one brief glance before resuming their laser-focused surveillance of the breakfast preparation.

Coming up behind her, he slid his hands around her waist.

She jumped, nearly dropping the spatula. The dogs leapt to attention.

"Jesse! Don't sneak up on me like that!"

He pulled her closer, kissing the exposed nape of her neck. "Couldn't resist." Craning his head around her, he scanned the food, making appreciative noises. "What did I do to deserve this?"

She wriggled away, giggling as she brandished her utensils. "Stop distracting me!" Checking the golden bottom of a pancake, she blew out a breath. "I wanted to surprise you with breakfast in bed," she admitted, glancing back at him. "You always spoil me, so I wanted to do something for you."

His heart stumbled. "You didn't need to do that. But I have to admit, it smells incredible."

"It does? Oh, good. I didn't exactly spend a lot of time cooking in what passed for kitchens in New York apartments, but it's coming back to me." She slid a trio of pancakes onto a waiting plate. "Here you go. I found some butter and syrup... it's on the island."

He snagged a few strips of bacon and added them to his plate. As he brewed a cup of coffee, his gaze wandered out the kitchen windows. Along the edge of the woods, tinges of yellow and orange broke into the sea of dark green. Crisp air drifted through the screens. Autumn was approaching. He felt that familiar pang associated with the end of summer, and he glanced back at Lark. Would the change in seasons herald a change in their relationship?

She joined him at the kitchen table, and they tucked into breakfast, the dogs shuffling at their feet. As she sipped the last of her orange juice, she caught his gaze, biting down on her lip. "I've been thinking a lot. About where we go from here."

His chest tightened, but he forced levity into his voice. "Back to bed?"

"You're insatiable," she said with a laugh, a blush blooming on her cheeks. "Not that I'm complaining." Her expression turned serious as she rose from the table to stack their plates. "I meant...the future."

He caught her wrist, pulling her down onto his lap. "I know what you meant. I've been thinking about it, too. And there's something I need to tell you."

She stiffened, a range of emotions playing across her face. Her pulse fluttered in her neck as she pulled in a shaky breath.

He couldn't tell if she was hopeful, apprehensive, scared, or some combination. But he had to reveal the depth of his feelings. And he had to share what he'd decided.

He cupped her face, sliding his thumb over her cheek. "I'm in love with you, Lark."

Her eyes widened, sparkling with joy. A smile lit up her features as she threw her arms around his neck. "I love you too." She melted into him, the tension seeping from her body. "I've been afraid to say the words, but I do. I love you."

He held her tightly, rubbing her back. "Good. Because I don't want to be apart from you. I know you want to go back to New York at some point, so I've been thinking about finding someone else to run the clinic. So I could go with you. I'm sure they have vets in New York City."

"What?" She drew back, her brows lifting as she stared at him. "But...you promised your father you'd keep it going."

He *had* promised, and going back on his word would hurt him. But he had to believe his father would understand the need to follow his heart. When he'd made that promise, he hadn't really considered a situation in which he'd need to move away. On some subconscious level, he'd just assumed that his future partner would want to live here. Most year-round residents thought of Truro as paradise, but they were biased—they'd already made the choice to make this their home.

Love was about compromise; about putting someone else's needs ahead of your own. His parents had demonstrated that throughout their marriage, and they would expect Jesse to do the same. If his future took him somewhere else, he'd just have to do his best to find someone willing to buy the practice. It probably wouldn't be easy—it didn't make a huge profit—but there were other reasons another vet might be willing to step in and take over. He'd do what he could to honor his father's wishes by trying to keep the clinic open, and that would have to be enough. Because being around Lark had made him realize that home wasn't just about a geographic place. Wherever he and Lark chose to live would be home, as long as they were together.

He cleared his throat. "My dad would understand. The clinic meant a lot to him, but not more than my happiness."

"And being with me makes you happy?" She blinked as moisture glistened in her eyes.

"It does. I miss you when I'm not with you. You're the first person I want to talk to in the morning, and the first person I want to see when I'm done at work. There's been a connection between us since we first met. I never really believed in fate, but I feel like you were brought here for a reason."

She cocked her head. "Aside from solving a ghost mystery, you mean?"

"See?" he said, chuckling. "You're always able to make me laugh, too."

Her melodic laughter joined his for a moment before she grew serious again. "I felt the connection from the day we met, too. I just didn't want to trust in it, after everything I'd been through. I had decided never to fall in love again, but with you, well...there was no decision to be made. I just fell."

"I'm glad. I know it wasn't easy. But I'll never hurt you, Lark."

"I believe you. I trust you, and I trust us." She shifted her weight, dropping her gaze before looking back at him. "But what I wanted to talk about...it wasn't about moving back to New York. Well, in a way it was, actually. I came to my own realization. The only reason I wanted to go back was to hold on to something familiar, after everything in my life shifted so drastically in such a short period of time. It almost felt like that was the last piece of my identity. But that's not true. You've made me see that, and being here has made me see that. Despite everything that happened, New York City holds some great memories for me. But I think that now, it's my past." Inhaling, she searched his face for his reaction.

"You don't want to go back?"

She shook her head.

A tentative spark of happiness ignited inside him, but her expression kept it from growing. Why did she look so torn?

"This is great news," he said carefully, tucking a stray lock of hair behind her ear. "But...did you think I wouldn't be happy?"

"Well, it's just..." She trailed off, swallowing hard before trying again. "I really like it here, and it doesn't hurt that the man I love is here either." Her lips curved into a small smile. "But this is a small town, and it's *your* hometown. I'm afraid that by staying here, I'm putting pressure on us. And on you. I just don't want it to seem like I have certain...expectations." Color bloomed on her cheeks as she fidgeted on his lap.

His muscles relaxed. "I would never think that, Lark. But I understand what you're saying." Pausing, he kissed her shoulder, searching for a way to reassure her. "I know it's a big step. But you're not putting pressure on me. Think about it this way —before you even mentioned moving here, I told you I wanted us to be together, wherever that was. Right?"

"Right." Relief rolled off of her as she exhaled. "And I'm overwhelmed that you would have been willing to come to New York with me. Especially since you love your job here, and you love running your family's clinic."

"I do. But like I said—I want us to be together."

She nodded. "I do, too. And I'm glad we can do that here. The residents here need you. Preston might have died if you weren't available in the middle of the night." A shiver traveled through her. "I'm grateful for your dedication, and I know all the residents and vacationers who've needed your help are too. Your dedication to the clinic is one of the things I love about you."

"And your strength is one of the things I love about you.

You've been through a lot of loss, and starting over in a new town isn't easy. You're sure about this?"

"Yes. This is a beautiful place, and I own a house that's both rent-free and, now, ghost-free." She shot him a wry smile. "And I like the people I work with, although that job might not be enough to keep the lights on. But I've been thinking about joining that co-op in Provincetown I told you about. Trying to sell some prints. It might not add much to my income, but it's something I love."

"You should definitely do it, then. The rest will sort itself out. Plus, I'm here to help you. Although I know how much you hate that."

She pressed her lips together to hold back her laughter. "I'm getting better at it. It's not a terrible thing to depend on someone, especially when it's someone you know you can count on."

His heart contracted, and he ran a knuckle gently over her cheek. "I'm glad you feel that way."

"Well, you did save my life," she pointed out, one of her shoulders lifting in a playful shrug.

"The things you make me do to prove myself," he joked. Shaking his head, he tightened his arm around her waist. "God, I hate thinking about that night. I can't believe I almost lost you."

A span of silence filled the room as memories crashed around them. When Lark spoke, her voice rang with emotion. "In everything that happened, though, we found each other. And we found peace for Eva."

The extent of everything that had happened, both in the last few weeks and in the last few minutes, sank in as they remained locked in an embrace. "I love you," she whispered, burying her face in his neck.

"I love you, too." He ran his hand along the outside of her thigh. After a few beats, he added, "What did you want to do today?"

"Well, I need to clean up in here."

"Nope," he said firmly. "You cooked, I'll clean up."

She made an appreciative noise, nuzzling her way up toward his ear. "Yeah?"

Her warm breath against his neck quickened his pulse. "Absolutely. But, maybe not right this second." His fingers continued to slide over her smooth skin.

"No? Did you have something else in mind first?"

His breath caught as she nibbled on his earlobe. Desire flooded through him in a potent rush. "I have some ideas," he conceded, his voice rough.

"Hmm," she murmured as she adjusted her position on his lap, wrapping her legs around to straddle him. "Like...errands?"

He slipped his hands beneath her shirt, fanning her ribcage. "Not what I was thinking."

She scooted forward, pushing her hips closer. "Grocery store?" Her lips moved slowly down the length of his neck.

He shook his head wordlessly as his thumbs grazed her nipples.

"Guess we could go for a walk..." She trailed off, making a low sound in her throat as she rocked against him, her bottom pressing into his erection.

He groaned, reaching down in one swift movement to grip

the backs of her thighs. Shoving the chair back from the table, he stood up with her in his arms, and she let out a sultry laugh. She clung to him, her legs wrapped around his waist, as he carried her toward the stairs.

———

THE SKY STRETCHED into an endless arc of blackness, its canvas scattered with the brilliance of countless stars glowing from distant realms. Lark snuggled next to Jesse on the blanket they'd brought down to the beach as she gazed upward. The rhythmic tumble and retreat of the waves was the only sound, a soothing backdrop to the otherwise perfect stillness. She couldn't believe this was the first time she was doing this since she'd been here.

It had been Jesse's idea. After they'd actually done a few errands this morning—early afternoon, really—he'd put on the local news while they were preparing dinner. A small meteor shower was forecasted for tonight, and Jesse suggested they head down to the beach to stargaze. It was past ten o'clock, and he had to work in the morning, but they'd napped a little after falling back into bed. And it seemed like the perfect way to end the day they'd both uttered—and received—those three magical words.

They'd also marked the day by choosing an inscription for Eva's headstone. They'd found a church in Wellfleet willing to donate a cemetery plot, and they wanted to be ready when her remains were finally released. They wanted something that would also quietly honor the unborn child only they knew about, so they'd decided on a quote from Matthew: "Blessed are the pure in heart, for they shall see God."

They'd made the selection while over at her house, so they could also spend time with Preston. She felt a little guilty about spending every night over at Jesse's, but when they lived in New York, she'd been away from the apartment for more than eight hours during the day, and he'd been fine. With the ghost at peace, he seemed quite content to move about the spacious house to find various spots to nap. And she kept the bird-feeders full so he could watch the constant activity from his perch.

When Jesse had made an offhand remark about her and Preston moving in with him someday, her heart had swelled for the hundredth time that day, but she'd reminded him he had two dogs. He'd laughed and pointed out that as a veteri-narian, he was pretty good with animals. "All it takes is time, patience, and a lot of tuna fish," he'd assured her.

Overhead, a meteor shot across the sky, and she gasped, clutching his hand. "Did you see it?"

"I did. There goes another one," he said, gesturing with his free hand toward the streak of light.

She kept her eyes trained overhead, completely mesmer-ized by the celestial show. With no electric lights to dull the effect, and no buildings or clouds to block the view, the vast-ness of the night sky was overwhelming. Breathtaking.

"This is amazing. It sort of feels like we're at the edge of the world."

He chuckled softly. "Well, we're close." Shifting to his side, he brushed a kiss against her temple. "Don't forget to make a wish."

She shivered with pleasure at the warmth of his breath against her ear. Somehow, her wishes seemed to have all come true. The pieces of her life had come back together, even stronger. She had a new home, new friendships, and a new opportunity to rekindle her passion for photography. Best of all, her heart no longer felt like a fragile piece of glass, lined with cracks. It was whole now. Complete. Filled with joy, contentment, and indescribable love for the man beside her.

She turned toward him, stealing a glance at his handsome profile. "My wishes have been granted," she said, her voice weighted with the sincerity of her words and reverence for this night.

Lifting their joined fingers, he kissed the back of her hand. "Mine, too."

ACKNOWLEDGMENTS

I'm truly grateful for my readers, so thanks to everyone who came on Lark and Jesse's journey in Ghost Moon. Your support means the world to me, and when I hear from a satisfied reader—whether via email, social media, or a review—it absolutely makes my day. Please do consider leaving a short review, it really helps a book gain visibility!

I could never have written any of my novels without the love and encouragement of my husband, so thank you, Chris. I love you. Thank you to my friend and enthusiastic Beta reader Kathy. Thanks to my gym ladies who help keep me fit (and sane). Thanks to my amazing cover artist, author K.R. Conway. Thank you to readers Alicia H. and Maritza F. for naming Dr. Holt's dogs. And to all my family and friends, thank you for the incredible support of my books, and for the love, friendship, and support throughout the years. I love and appreciate you all.

ABOUT THE AUTHOR

USA TODAY Bestselling Author Kathryn Knight writes books filled with steamy romance, dangerous secrets, and haunting mysteries. Her novels are award-winning #1 Amazon and B&N Bestsellers and RomCon Reader-Rated picks. When she's not reading or writing, Kathryn spends her time exploring abandoned places and searching for ghosts. She lives on beautiful Cape Cod with her husband, their two sons, and a number of rescued pets. Please visit her at www.kathrynknightbooks.blogspot.com.

AMAZON AUTHOR PAGE

THE HAUNTING OF HILLWOOD FARM

EXCERPT

Chapter One

The sugar bowl slid across the kitchen counter, its lid rattling with jerky bursts of motion. Alice Turner froze, her fingers clenched around the mug of coffee she held suspended in midair, a curl of steam wavering in the sudden chill. Goosebumps prickled her skin as she stared at the yellow ceramic bowl, zigzagging its way toward her via some unseen force. It jittered to a halt directly in front of her, and her taut muscles went limp. Her coffee mug slammed down against the dark stone countertop, sending scalding liquid sloshing over her hand. She cried out, more from fright than pain, and stumbled back, nearly tripping as her foot slid out of its slipper. The near fall sent another bolt of panic through her. At 73, she was still quite active, but a broken bone would put an end to that.

She steadied herself. *Careful.* Blowing out a breath, she glanced at the reddening skin of her hand before quickly returning her gaze to the wayward bowl. *Had it really just moved on its own?* Despite the fear coursing through her veins, a wave of relief washed over her.

Maybe she *wasn't* losing her mind. Maybe all her recent worries about dementia, fueled by things like finding objects someplace other than where she'd left them, or discovering kitchen drawers open when she was sure she'd closed them, were unfounded. Could some kind of...supernatural phenomenon be responsible? A shiver crawled up her spine. That alternative wasn't a particularly comforting thought. And her practical New England roots didn't exactly lend themselves to that line of reasoning.

She cradled her throbbing hand against her chest, studying the sugar bowl for more movement. But it seemed to have completed its journey and had now reverted to an inanimate object, ready and waiting to sweeten her coffee.

With cautious steps, she backed away from the counter, crossing the kitchen toward the sink. Flipping on the faucet, she held her injured hand under the stream of cold water.

Was she really considering the presence of a ghost? It would help to explain all the strange occurrences she'd noticed since she'd returned from her trip. Without Henry. A deep ache flared in her chest as her gaze cut over to the chair he used to settle in at the big farmhouse table, empty now. With a heavy sigh, she glanced back at the stationary bowl as she dried her hand with a checkered dish towel.

It *had* moved. She was certain. Retrieving her mug, she

nodded forcefully, trying to push away the pinpricks of doubt threatening to erode her conviction. Either a spirit had manipulated the sugar bowl, or she was truly cracking up. The latter theory felt like the more terrifying one. She didn't even want to contemplate the possibility that her ties to sanity, already frayed by grief, had finally snapped, and hallucinations were her new reality.

Maybe it was time to talk to Luke, to see if he'd noticed anything unusual since he'd been living with her at Hillwood. It was just that he was already so worried about her. As much as she loved him, she didn't need a babysitter; nor did she want her 27-year-old grandson to have to take on that role. So far, their cohabitation was working out, but once he got a load of her sugar bowl story, that might change quickly.

Another pocket of frigid air swirled around her, and she spun around. Her gaze searched the empty kitchen and the back hallway. No one was there. She turned back slowly, her heart thumping in her ears. From her position behind the long counter separating the kitchen from the dining room, she could see the foyer. The front door remained shut. The windows were still closed against last night's rain. Besides that, it was 65 degrees outside, according to the thermometer in the window above the sink. A cold front inside the house made little sense, unless…

"Henry?" Her voice wavered in the silence.

The sugar bowl shivered slightly, as if a small earthquake had opened up beneath it. An extremely localized earthquake that had no effect on anything else nearby. Her trembling hands flew to her mouth as a potent mix of fear and longing swept through her. She slid her damp palms downward, over the hammering in her chest. "Is that you?" she added, the words barely emerging from her dusty throat.

The lights flickered. She glanced up, her breath catching. A soft moan rippled through the air, raising in pitch until it became a distant wail. She clutched the folds of her robe, every muscle in her body vibrating with tension. A sudden movement caught her eye, and she snapped her head back toward the sugar bowl as it careened off the counter, shattering in an explosion of ceramic shards and white powder.

Chapter Two

THE FARMHOUSE LOOKED COMPLETELY normal from the outside, if a little worse for the wear due to its age. According to Alice, the historic home in Sandwich, Massachusetts, had been in the Turner family not just for generations but for centuries, with parts of the original 1780s structure still intact amongst the additions and renovations completed over the years. A wide, welcoming porch, complete with Adirondack chairs, rockers, and hanging plants, stretched across the front of the home, wrapping around the sides. Old steel milk jugs flanked the red front door, and checkered curtains hung in the windows. Everything about it was quaint and inviting.

But Callie Sinclair felt it as soon as they climbed the worn wooden steps to the porch. *Something was here.* Sure enough, when Alice opened the front door and gestured her inside, the whispers began. They swirled through her head, a chorus of faraway voices rustling like tattered leaves in the wind, traveling through time and space, from who knew where.

Despite the warmth of the early May afternoon, a shiver slid through her, and she pulled her long, lightweight sweater coat around her chest, resisting the urge to try to close off her mind. She was here to listen, after all, and she could feel the nervous anticipation rolling off of Alice as they entered the foyer. The older woman had clearly been excited for her arrival; she'd met Callie in the long driveway, her silvery hair catching in the spring breeze as strands escaped the knot pinned loosely on the back of her head.

"Are you cold, dear?" The furrows lining Alice's forehead deepened. "Or do you...feel something?"

"Just a little chill," she said with a weak smile, purposefully keeping her answer vague. She did feel something beyond a mysterious chill in the air...but she didn't want to get Alice's hopes up. And it was difficult to explain. Of course there were remnants of past lives lingering here; it was pretty much a given for any home with this type of history. Many people connected to this house would have passed on over the years, leaving some imprint of their essence, like the blurred images captured beneath closed eyelids after a bright flash.

But she was here to connect with someone specific: Henry Turner. Alice had sought Callie out upon hearing about her abilities from a mutual acquaintance. When Callie had reluctantly agreed to meet Alice at a coffee shop last week, she'd taken pity on the kind widow. How could she not? Alice and Henry had been married 53 years, and they had saved up to finally afford their dream vacation—a 28-day Polynesian cruise. When Henry had suffered a massive heart attack in the middle of the South Pacific Ocean, the medical personnel on board had not been able to save him.

But after the funeral, when things began settling down at the normally quiet farmhouse, Alice started noticing strange occurrences, which increased in frequency and severity as the weeks went by. She now firmly believed her late husband was trying to tell her something—and that his message was urgent.

Callie hadn't wanted to get involved, but Alice truly seemed to believe she—or someone she loved—might be in danger, and contact with Henry was the key to possibly preventing tragedy. Either Alice was genuinely concerned, or she was an excellent actress... but Callie couldn't see the point in making a story like that up, considering Alice would be paying her money for her services. When Alice's pleas were joined by barely contained tears, Callie relented.

And now, here she was. In an isolated old farmhouse, with a woman she really didn't know, searching for a ghost.

While she could hear the lingering murmurs of long-gone souls, she couldn't make out anything distinct. So far, there was no bright spark of connection to a specific person, like she'd experienced before. But maybe she just needed to give it time. What did she know about the process, really? The few times it had happened to her, the spirits had come to her, on their own, and had plagued her with a determined tenacity until she opened her mind up to the messages and relayed them to the intended recipients. If there was a process she was supposed to go through, she had no idea what it was. She had no degree in this type of thing, no certification. It was just a bizarre and unwelcome result of the accident.

"I feel it from time to time too," Alice said, a knowing look gleaming in her pale blue eyes. She closed the front door to block the air coming in through the screen door and nodded toward the kitchen. "How about a cup of hot coffee? Or tea?"

"I never say no to coffee," she said gratefully, playing with the long dragonfly pendant around her neck. That was true, although she'd probably had enough already this morning at her apartment.

She was starting to think coming here was a mistake. But Alice had been so desperate, and Callie herself knew how comforting a message from beyond could be. That first time, though, right after the accident, she'd thought she was losing her mind. But then it started happening again, whenever she was with Karen, her physical therapist, and she finally gathered up the nerve to ask her if she had a sister who'd died recently. And the answer, sadly, had been a surprised 'yes'. Once Callie began relaying the phrases echoing through her head, things Karen confirmed only the twin sisters would have known, her new reality set in. And Karen avoided marrying the fiancé who was cheating on her. After a few more instances, Callie came to accept she was now some kind of conduit between two worlds—but she'd never actively sought the connection before. Maybe if you tried to force it, it wouldn't come.

Still playing with her necklace, a gift from her father, she followed Alice into the house. The floorplan was open on either side of the central staircase, with a welcoming family room to the left; they walked to the right, through an airy dining area that transitioned into the kitchen. The décor was a mix of country charm and seaside accents, a nod to both their rural homestead and its location on Cape Cod, a peninsula surrounded by water. Old signs advertising fruits and vegetables for sale hung on the pale yellow walls, and canning jars filled with shells sat on the windowsills.

Part of the counter top extended out in an L-shape between the kitchen and dining spaces, and Callie leaned against it, admiring an antique-looking iron rooster tucked in the corner. *Did they have hens here?* Fresh eggs every morning would be such a luxury. She'd noticed a few other buildings at the bottom of the hill beyond the house, one of which looked like a barn. But the only animal she'd seen thus far was a large black cat, sitting on a post of a split rail fence and eyeing her with contempt.

"I know it's the afternoon already, but is a breakfast blend okay?" Alice asked as she filled the coffee pot in the deep white sink. "My grandson likes the stronger stuff, so I do have dark roast."

"Breakfast blend sounds wonderful."

Alice measured the coffee, then gestured with the little metal scoop toward where Callie stood. "That's where the sugar bowl slid off the counter and smashed."

Her gaze found a new sugar bowl, next to a napkin holder resembling chicken wire, and Callie stared at it for a moment, as if history might repeat itself.

Alice retrieved two mugs from an overhead cabinet. "I know it sounds crazy, but I saw it with my own two eyes, even if they are old eyes."

"I believe you." She reached for the sugar bowl herself, moving it within easy reach. "Is there anything I can do to help?"

Alice waved her offer away as she crossed to the fridge and pulled out a jug of milk. "No, no, just make yourself comfortable." She poured some milk into a small white pitcher and picked up the thread of the previous conversation. "Even if I'd had any doubt about it moving on its own, I sure didn't imagine cleaning up all the mess after it flew off the edge and hit the floor."

Callie nodded as she pulled a stool from under the counter. "That must have been a frustrating way to start the morning."

"The thing is…why would Henry want to make me have to clean up a big mess?" Alice set the milk pitcher next to the sugar bowl, locking her gaze with Callie's. Her thin lips pressed into a seam, turning the soft folds of skin around her mouth into parenthesis. The coffee maker sputtered and gurgled in the background. "He was always telling me I was doing too much around here, after I hurt my shoulder. I mean, we had disagreements on occasion, just like any couple, but I have no doubt he loved me. In the 53 years we were together, he was never mean-spirited or cruel."

Callie frowned, a small sound of acknowledgement

emerging from the back of her throat. It was an interesting observation, but she certainly didn't have the answer. *Go on, then, Henry...explain. I'm listening.*

"When it first started moving, a small part of my brain thought, 'He's trying to help me, to pass the sugar'. It was scary, but a little sweet. But then when it suddenly smashed like that, it felt...different. Not sweet anymore. It felt...angry."

"I'm sure it's hard for a spirit to move something in the physical world. Maybe he just...doesn't have a lot of control over it," she offered, shifting on her stool as she gathered her dark curtain of hair over her shoulder and coiled it into a rope.

Alice tilted her head to the side, considering. "Well, he certainly got my attention, if that was the point. And then there were all the other things that have happened that I told you about last week. The family pictures that fell and shattered after years of hanging on the same wall. A huge crack appearing in my car's windshield when it was safely in the garage. All the laundry I'd hung on the clothesline ending up on the ground. Important papers going missing." She ticked off each incident on her thin fingers, the gold band on her left hand catching the light from the fixture overhead. With a small shrug, she added, "Anyway, all this was enough to convince me to find someone who could help, that's for sure." She nodded toward Callie before turning back toward the coffee maker.

Of course, it remained to be seen whether she could actually be any help. A surge of nervous energy hummed through her, and she ordered herself to relax. There was no real pressure here; she had signed no contract, received no money.

She'd only agreed to come by the house for an initial visit, and go from there.

Danger. The word rustled in her head, thick and muffled, as though coming from underwater. But it wasn't her thought, and it was accompanied by that familiar flare of pressure in her skull. She froze, her eyes searching the room. She'd never actually seen a ghost, but the instinct to look for a figure to go with a disembodied voice was tough to ignore.

Nothing but the back of Alice's thin but surprisingly sturdy frame as she filled two coffee mugs on the other side of the kitchen. Cropped tan pants, untucked powder blue blouse, pewter strands of hair still vying for freedom from the loose bun.

She turned her head slowly. Just the vacant farm table, the empty foyer, and a partial view of the front door, still closed.

A tremor shuddered through her. So...a connection had been made, even if briefly. And the message—*danger*—was not exactly comforting. Knitting her brows, she strained to pick up something else. But it was just the background noise of whispers now, slowly fading away like a battery draining of power. Those spirits had no real reason to reach her, no unfinished business keeping them caught between worlds. They only wanted someone to know they'd been here, once, and had left a tiny piece of their presence behind. The memory of a life lived.

Ghosts who moved things in the physical world and sought out mediums, in her experience anyway, had something important to relay. And the fact that someone—Alice?—was in danger...well, that felt important. Callie realized she was stuck now. How could she refuse to help if danger lurked around this sweet woman?

The thud of footsteps on the porch jolted her from her ruminations, and she jumped in her seat, the word *danger* still rattling through her mind.

THE HAUNTING OF HILLWOOD FARM on Kindle